# After the Fortune Cookies

# After the
# Fortune Cookies

*Ann R. Blakeslee*

———

G. P. Putnam's Sons, New York

G.P. Putnam's Sons, a division of
The Putnam & Grosset Group, 200 Madison Avenue,
New York, NY 10016.
Published simultaneously in Canada
Printed in the United States of America
Book design by Christy Hale
Library of Congress Cataloging-in-Publication Data
Blakeslee, Ann R. After the fortune cookies /
Ann R. Blakeslee.
p.   cm. Summary: The summer Allison turns
twelve brings many disturbing changes, as she
fights to protect her beloved grandfather from the
schemes of other family members and seeks the
courage to stand up to the taunts of her
spiteful cousin Carolina.
ISBN 0-399-21562-x
[1. Cousins—Fiction.   2. Grandfathers—Fiction.
3. Family life—Fiction.   4. Self-confidence—Fiction.]   I. Title.
PZ7.B577Af   1989 [Fic]—dc20   89-33401 CIP AC
1   3   5   7   9   10   8   6   4   2
First Impression

For CHUCK
who is my common sense, courage, and joy
and For ELIZABETH

# Contents

# 1

## The Double Birthday Party

First it was my cousin Carolina's turn. She blew out the twelve candles on her birthday cake with a whoosh and a whistle that made the adults smile. Then it was my turn. I looked at the lighted candles in front of me and said, "I wish I could stay eleven forever. Eleven was perfect."

My Aunt Bee sighed and shifted in her chair. "Allison, you make me tired. You say that same thing every birthday. Ten was perfect. Nine was perfect. If you are going to be a strong, forceful adult, you will have to stop looking backward and start to grow up."

Grandfather squeezed my hand as if to make up for Aunt Bee's sharp words. August heat was steaming up the dining room, but his hand felt cold. "Is that true?" I asked him. "Do I say it every year?"

"You do," he said, smiling. "I've never known anyone to cling to her happy childhood times as you do."

I glanced around the dinner table to see if the rest of the family agreed. There really aren't many of us, but we confuse people until we're sorted out. We're three generations of Godolphins. Grandfather is oldest. His children, Aunt Bee, Uncle Robert, and Mama come next. And the cousins, Robby, Carolina, and I are the third. Newcomers in Godolphinville, where we live, always ask about us because the town is named for my family.

Mama and Daddy smiled at Grandfather, agreeing with what he'd said. So did Uncle Robert. Robby winked at me. He's always on my side. But Carolina gave me a hard look. "You didn't think eleven was so perfect when you crashed down the library steps on Robby's skateboard. Or when you were the only girl in our class not invited to Melody's party. Or when—"

"That will do, Carolina. Let Bygones Be Bygones." Aunt Bee delivers maxims as if she's just made them up. It silences people, even her own daughter, Carolina.

I looked again at the candles on my cake. Their yellow wax was melting onto the lemon icing. Twelve candles was too many. Twelve would mean catching the school bus at six A.M. for the Consolidated Junior High over in Luxor, and not getting home till late. It meant leaving Robby behind at Godolphinville Elementary, and spending less time with Grandfather. I wasn't ready for twelve.

"We are waiting." My aunt clicked her spoon against her plate.

"You want some help, Al?" Robby asked. I nodded. He came and stood beside me and we blew out the candles. The way everyone sang "Happy Birthday" off-key made me smile instead of crying.

The combined birthday party is one of our family rituals. Carolina and I have celebrated our August birthdays together at my house ever since we had our one-year-old cakes on our highchair trays. Being first cousins and practically the same age, everyone thought we'd grow up best friends. But we're too different. She's beautiful and snooty, and her crowd rules our class at school. I'm just her tomboy cousin. Carolina isn't into tomboys these days and she doesn't let me forget it.

"Girls, pay attention." Aunt Bee was holding out boxes to each of us. I knew what would be in them, twin dresses to wear to the Godolphinville town reunion. She gives us the same thing every year. She does it so people will recognize us as the two Godolphin granddaughters. The dresses she picks are always frilly. They're fine on Carolina. But I still have my baby fat and look like a ruffled sofa cushion in mine.

Carolina was holding her dress up looking doubtfully at

it. The pink color made you notice her black, black hair and rose-petal skin. The dress was the same fussy kind Aunt Bee always gives us with a big bow in the back. I wondered why Carolina wasn't whirling around, showing it off like she has every other year.

The family turned to watch me unwrap my box. I hated to open it and pretend to be pleased, but there was no use stalling. I gave Aunt Bee a quick thank-you kiss, wishing I could tell her what I thought. I'm a regular spook in pink.

Mama's and Daddy's gifts were next. They were dress boxes, just alike again. "To save for your first day of Junior High," Mama said.

My heart sank. Had she chosen twin dresses for us to wear to school? But when the packages were opened I stammered with relief, "I love it." Mine was a wrap-around plaid skirt, mostly brown. A plain tan pullover went with it. My style. The one for Carolina was her style, too, a blousy top and tight pants to match in yellow, red, and orange stripes.

Robby and his dad, Uncle Robert, brought kazoos for everyone. When Aunt Bee saw what was in the awkward little bundles, she laid hers down unopened. The rest of us tootled scales, then louder and sillier, "Jingle Bells." Then with harmony, standing up, "The Star Spangled Banner," though Mama laughed so hard she had to sit down in the middle.

"Who can beat me tap dancing while playing the kazoo?" Daddy asked. No one got up to challenge him. He did the shuffle to "New York, New York," slim and bald and graceful like Fred Astaire, but taller. We sang along. Daddy's always fun.

Mama teased him. "You're wasted traveling around the world selling Godolphin's Fine Furniture. You should be starring on Broadway."

He rubbed his hand across her cheek. "If that wasn't your best lace cloth I'd have danced on the table."

"Do it. Do it, Uncle Peter," Robby shouted. But Aunt Bee squashed that idea. She has a way of patting her perfectly arranged black hair when she's impatient. She patted till we quieted down.

Grandfather's presents are always books out of his own library. But this year he surprised us. He pulled a big package from behind the dining room door and carried it to Carolina. "There's a lesson I want to teach you, Carolina. I hope this will help you learn it." As soon as she opened his gift I could see it pleased her. That shine came on her that makes people enjoy watching her. She gave me a look as if to say, "I bet you're jealous."

"What is it?" Mama asked.

Carolina turned Grandfather's present around so we could see. There were ooohs of surprise. He had given her the painting of our Grandmother Katy Rose, who was so special to all of us before she died. With it propped in her lap I could see how much my cousin's getting to look like our beautiful Grandmother used to. "You resemble Katy

Rose so closely, Carolina," Grandfather said. "I hope each day you'll grow more like her."

Carolina called, "Thanks, Grandfather," down the long table and blew him a kiss. She snapped on the wall lights and set the painting on the sideboard behind Aunt Bee.

"I'd forgotten how much you look like Grandmother, Bee," Uncle Robert said.

Aunt Bee answered, "We were cut from the same pattern, Grandmother, Carolina, and I." But everybody smiles when they remember Grandmother Katy Rose because she was so sweet. Sometimes Aunt Bee and Carolina are as sour as lemon juice.

Grandfather lifted a second package from behind the door and set it on the table in front of me. "There's a lesson I want to teach you, too, Allison. It's different from Carolina's. This should help you with it."

"What lessons do you want them to learn?" Robby asked, his green eyes shiny as candles. He loves a mystery.

"I think the girls will guess. But if they don't, they'll find their lessons written in their fortune cookies." Uh-oh, I thought, he wants to improve our characters.

The fortune cookie dinner is when Grandfather tells us if he thinks someone needs to shape up. He gives the dinner the Saturday before school starts, which is also the day of the town reunion. At dessert time, besides our pie, we each open a fortune cookie. There aren't Chinese sayings inside. Grandfather slides those out and puts his own in. We get congratulations or stern advice depending on how he thinks we've done the past year. Even parents get them. Nobody tells what Grandfather wrote. But sometimes we know by each others' faces which kind people got. It sure takes the flavor out of dessert when you get a bad one.

I unwrapped Grandfather's gift. There weren't words to say how I felt when I saw what was in the big package. He had given me the thing I loved most in his house, my grandmother's clock. I hugged him as hard as I could.

We all knew the story of how he bought the clock, but he told us again. "Before we were married, I saw this in the window of Marshall Field's store in Chicago. Because of the painted frame with its carved leaves and flowers, and the climbing roses on the pendulum, I wanted it for Katy Rose."

"Don't forget to tell how you got the money to buy it," Robby said.

"I had to take a second job, at night, to pay for it. That was back when I was a young professor and my salary wasn't enough. But before our wedding day, I owned the clock. Your grandmother loved it, Allison. I hope you will, too."

I slid my hands across the painted wooden flowers. Even when I was tiny I thought that clock was wonderful. I remember Grandmother holding me up so I could touch the carving. The last thing I've always done before I leave Grandfather's house is go into the living room to watch the rose-covered pendulum swing.

"Read out what it says around the clock face," Grandfather said.

The gold writing was so tiny and the letters so twisted

together, I'd always thought they were just a design. Now, close up, I could see it said something. It wasn't easy unscrambling one curly letter from the next. But at last I figured it out and spoke it slowly, "There is a tide, which taken at the flood, leads on to fortune."

I wish I hadn't looked up then. At the other end of the table Carolina, her shine gone, was throwing me the secret look we've used since we were small. It means, Want to trade? Often out behind the bushes we've swapped gifts when our party was over. I didn't blame her; who wouldn't want the clock? But she spoiled the birthday magic like she'd spoiled so many other things for me that summer.

I shook my head feeling selfish but lucky, wishing there were two clocks. Carolina was probably wishing the same thing. If so, it was the first time in weeks we'd agreed on anything.

# 2

## *Introducing the Nose*

Outside the dining room windows it had turned dark. Fireflies flashed their tiny lights advertising just how dark it was. We cut our cakes and Mama brought the ice cream. The birthday party was nearly over. By the calendar I was twelve years old. But I didn't feel like it. In a little more than two weeks I'd start Junior High. I wasn't ready for that.

Robby and I asked to be excused. We went into the dim living room and kicked our shoes into a corner, throwing our socks after them. Even though he's only ten I'd rather be with him than Carolina anytime. He flopped down on the floor and switched on the TV. I didn't want to watch. "It's different when you get to be twelve," I told him. "Things start to change and I hate changes. I wanted it always to stay the same, you and me going to Grandfather's house after school every day."

"Me, too."

"I knew those times were over when we blew out my candles."

"Uh-huh."

"And I'm worried about going over to Luxor to Junior High. What if Carolina and her friends tease me over there the way they have this summer over here? She'll make everybody think I'm awful before they have time to find out I'm okay."

That time Robby didn't answer. He sat still as a stone in front of the TV, his skin all summer brown, dark hair down over his thin face, his knees and elbows scratched and bruised. Maybe he couldn't hear me above the noise of the chase on the screen. I talked louder. "Are you listening to me or to the television?"

"Both. One ear each."

"I need you to listen just to me." He watched the police surround the bank robber, then snapped the sound off and turned around. The pictures still moved beside him.

"Mama gave me one of her serious talks this afternoon," I said. "She made me swear I wouldn't tell anybody a word she said."

"I don't think she meant me, do you?"

"She couldn't have. She knows I tell you everything."

"Well? Was it mushy?"

"No, just . . . I don't know. She said now that I'm twelve she's going to depend on me more. I'm supposed to start helping her keep peace in the family. She said Aunt Bee's giving Carolina a hard time even though Carolina isn't doing anything really wrong. She's just acting the way girls act when they want to grow up but their mothers aren't ready to let them."

"Why won't she let her?"

"That's what I asked and Mama sort of tried not to tell me. But I think Aunt Bee was a wild teenager. She was so pretty everyone wanted to date her and it went to her head. So she expects Carolina to act the same way. And being a widow, she doesn't know how she'll handle her alone."

"I don't see what all that stuff has to do with you."

"Well, Mama feels sorry for Carolina because Aunt Bee's trying to keep her little when she isn't. So I'm supposed to treat Carolina especially nice."

"What about Carolina treating you specially nice? She's been awful to you for a whole month."

"I didn't tell Mama that because that isn't what I'm worried about most. When she took me off to talk, I thought she was going to warn me about the Godolphin nose. But she didn't say a word about it." It gave me chills to speak about the nose.

Robby stared at my face head on. Then he said, "Turn so I can see you from the side." I turned and he looked at me that way. "I can't see that it's starting to grow, Al. Maybe it isn't going to." I never have to explain to Robby. He guesses how I feel and tries to help. He touched his own nose. "I suppose it's easier when you're born with it like me."

I looked at his profile against the flickering blue of the TV screen. His nose thrust out, a smaller model of Grandfather's and Uncle Robert's, two sharp sides of a triangle. On men it's fine. People talk about the "distinguished Godolphin nose." But poor Mama has it, too, a huge bird beak that started getting that way when she was in Junior High. Luckily she's such an easy, warm person, nobody cares how she looks.

I said, "You know tonight when Aunt Bee said that about me growing up to be a strong, forceful adult? All I could picture was me with the strong, forceful Godolphin nose. What will I do if mine starts growing? Everything else seems to change when people get to be twelve."

"I'll like you even if it gets as long as Pinocchio's."

"I know, Robby, but that doesn't count. Carolina will really have something to tease me about if I start growing the nose."

Grandfather came just then and stood in the doorway, a tall, stooped silhouette. So if Robby had other comforting things to say, he forgot them. "Anybody want to walk me home?" Grandfather asked.

That's another family ritual. He lives right next door, but Robby and I always see him home. While we walk, he teaches us poetry. He has a headful of it left over from when

20

he was an English professor. Through the years we've memorized so many poems we could probably recite more than all the teachers in our school put together.

That night we went the long way, around a couple of blocks. "A twelfth birthday should have a special quotation," Grandfather said, "one full of wisdom. Let's learn the verse from Shakespeare that's on Katy Rose's clock. There's more to it than the clock carver had space for."

He leaned against a lightpost. The brightness made his hair a silver halo and his kind face all dark hollows. His voice sounded like an actor's:

> " 'There is a tide in the affairs of men
> Which, taken at the flood, leads on to fortune;
> Omitted, all the voyage of their life
> Is bound in shallows and in miseries.' "

We walked along, trying to repeat the words. It was harder than learning something that rhymes. I thought we'd never get it right. As we crossed Q Street we were still completely muddled, mixing the lines all up, laughing at each other's mistakes. "What does 'taken at the flood' mean?" Robby asked.

"To begin something at the right time. Sailing captains used to leave harbor when the tide was flooding. Flooding means going out. They did that so the water would carry the ship with it."

"The same as flying a kite when the wind's up?" Robby asked. Kite flying is one of his favorite things.

"Yes. That's a good way to explain it."

We were getting most of the lines by the time we passed under the mulberry tree out in front of Miss Betty Willson's house. When Grandfather heard the swing creaking on her porch, he stopped to say hello.

The new preacher from Miss Betty's church was calling on her. She brought him to the steps to introduce us. He was halfway through a frozen chocolate eclair and stood there with the dessert plate balanced on one hand and a fork in the other. In spite of the cold dessert he looked hot and melted down in his black suit. Robby couldn't keep his eyes off the eclair, but Miss Betty didn't offer him one.

"I'm Reverend Kean," the preacher told Grandfather. "I hear this heat wave has the farmers worried about drought. I share their concern. Until it rains, I'm going to bend all my efforts toward praying up a storm." He laughed at his little joke and they said some more things grownups say to keep a conversation going. Then we walked on, my bare feet sliding on mulberries and Grandfather's slippers crunching them.

Robby said, "I nearly ran over that man with my bike after dark last night. I didn't see him from behind with his black hair and black clothes. He's been all around town this week, calling on people. I wonder if everyone feeds him fancy stuff like Miss Betty." Robby's always planned to be a famous comedian when he grows up. But right then he sounded like he was considering switching to being a minister.

To get his mind off it I asked Grandfather, "What does that line in the poem mean when it says 'bound in shallows'? I don't understand it." The truth was, I didn't understand most of the lines.

"If a captain missed the flood tide," he explained, "his ship got caught in shallow water. He had to wait for the tide to come in again and float it off. Shakespeare was saying life is the same way. When it's time to begin something, don't hang back."

We sat on the high curb where we always rest when Grandfather needs to catch his breath. Two kids in my class, John Amos and Pip Thatcher, rode their bikes down Front Street, winding in and out of the circles of light under the lampposts. Reflectors glittered on their wheels. John shouted, "Hi, you guys." But Pip just whistled one long note as he waved. It trailed out behind him and started all the dogs in the neighborhood barking.

We helped Grandfather to his feet and walked him across the street and up onto his high old porch. By the time we kissed him good night, we could both say the quotation all the way through. Nothing warned us that birthday night, sweet with honeysuckle and bright with fireflies doing acrobatics, what a lot of shallows and miseries were lying just ahead.

# 3

## *Calling Names*

When Grandfather went inside, Robby and I leaned on the porch railing to watch the heat lightning. Across Grandfather's gardens we saw that the birthday party had moved to the screened patio behind my house. The overhead lights made the family look like actors on a stage. Aunt Bee fluttered her hands as she talked, her gold bracelets twinkling. Opposite her Uncle Robert tipped back in his chair as if her words were washing him away. My parents sat on the couch close together, Mama's carrot-colored hair flaming against Daddy's blue sport shirt. Carolina stretched out in the corner with her feet on one chair and the rest of her on another.

Robby said, "Look at my poor dad leaning away from Aunt Bee like her words are pushing him over."

"They probably are. Have you ever known her that she wasn't pushing somebody? When I was in kindergarten I thought where my alphabet book said 'B is for Bulldozer,' it meant 'Bee is for Bulldozer.' "

"Al, that's perfect. From now on I'm going to call her The Bulldozer. Maybe I should give them all secret names. How about The Porcupine for Carolina, she's been so prickly lately?"

"Or Snow White," I said. "She really is the fairest in the land."

"But that's just her outside. Insides are what count."

"Maybe. But I'm learning it's outsides people see and decide on."

"You never worried about that before, Al."

"I know. But since I had my first really big fight with Carolina last month and she told me what a mess I am, I've been noticing how everyone compares me with her. You'll see what I mean when the great-aunts come for reunion. They ooh over Carolina. Then they look at me wondering where I fit on the family tree. I didn't used to mind. But I've started asking myself questions I never asked before. Like is this the right way for me to be?"

"Sure you're the right way. What's Carolina got that you haven't got?"

"That heavy hair she can do different things with, for one thing. Mine fights back when I try to make it lie down. She has those huge gray eyes and her eyelashes look painted. My eyes look pale and I have midget eyelashes. And any minute now I may start growing the nose."

Robby ignored what I said as if he didn't have an answer for it. "I've got to think up a name for your parents."

"No you don't. I named them to myself a long time ago. In August I call them The Dancers."

"What's August got to do with it?"

"The rest of the year they're just plain parents, busy and rushing. But in August when Daddy gets his vacation and doesn't keep running to Europe to sell furniture, and Mama takes off from her job at the factory, they have time to fall in love all over again. So I call them The Dancers."

"I still don't get it."

"You know those fifties movies on TV?" I asked him. "There's this dance place. Everybody's jitterbugging. Then the camera shows two people slow dancing in the corner, kind of in a dream. That's supposed to show they're very much in love. Mama and Daddy are like that in August."

"You never told me that."

"Well, it's kind of private. And they're still great and never yell at me. But if I ask something in August they don't really hear. They even forget to warn me about gumline cavities and brushing around my braces."

"One month a year isn't bad. My father doesn't hear me

26

most of the time because he's too busy running the factory. That's why I pretend Grandfather's my dad."

It always embarrasses us when we get to talking about the family's peculiar ways. This time wasn't any different. Tongue-tied, we started down Grandfather's steps to head home. But Pip and John came pedaling up Front Street from the direction of the stores. Their wheels hissed along the pavement. They squealed their bikes to a stop and John asked, "You guys want to ride around with us?"

"We can't. We're in the middle of my birthday party."

Robby asked them, "You been down at The Drug buying cinnamon balls?" He must have known they had. There was a cloud of cinnamon smell all around them.

"Yeah, but we ate them all," Pip said. "Climb on. We'll ride back and buy more. I still have money."

"Want to, Al? It won't take long. If we go home now someone will remember what time it is and send us to bed."

Before I could decide on an answer, two girls clattered down the steps of a house across the street. It was Carolina's best friend, Melody, and Lisa Pierce, who's a pain. When they saw us they began to snicker. They stepped to the curb, side by side, and started to kick and wave their arms like cheerleaders. Then they chanted:

"Allison, Allison, Allison dear
We ask you, we beg you

To just disappear,
Allison, Allison, Allison—UGH!"

I pretended I didn't know the girls were there. But inside me someone was crying, "Please, don't."

"You want us to shut them up for you?" Pip asked. "One sock and you'll never hear another word out of them."

"No. It's all part of a fight I had with Carolina. I'm the one who has to figure out how to stop it."

For a minute it was quiet under the tall elms that reached across the street to touch each other above our heads. Then Melody and Lisa began strutting and chanting again:

"Ally, Ally, Ally cat
Look at that
She's so fat,
Allison, Allison, Allison—UGH!"

They did cartwheels on UGH!

John and Pip put their heads together. They circled their bikes around and raced after the girls. Lisa and Melody started screaming. Dashing across the Pierces' lawn, they thudded up the porch steps. Mr. Pierce came to the window and glared out into the street.

Robby and I ran toward my patio, holding out our hands to feel the fireflies bounce against them. Our feet slid silently over the grass. He pulled me to a stop before we got close enough to be noticed. "Let's stay here and watch them until they whistle for us to come in."

We sat under the arch of the lilac bush. No one on the patio looked toward us. Daddy and Mama and Uncle Robert and Carolina were watching Aunt Bee. And we were watching them.

"We're the audience and they're the play," I whispered.

"Okay. If they say something funny, we'll clap and surprise them."

But it wasn't a comedy they were acting out on our patio. The Bulldozer was talking and she was deadly serious.

# 4

## *The Plot Against Grandfather*

Aunt Bee talks more than anybody else when she comes to our house. It makes me wonder if she saves up things to say. Now she was at the center of the stage and making the most of it. "And Grandfather came over here this evening in his bedroom slippers. Did you notice that? The past president of Godolphin's Fine Furniture Company walking down Front Street in broad daylight half dressed! He had a button off his shirt, too. And spots, like decorations, down his tie. What will people think?" She fanned herself with a *National Geographic.*

Nobody said anything. It's best to let The Bulldozer run on

for a while before you start to argue. "He is letting the family home fall into disrepair, too. There are shingles off his roof. A board is gone from the back fence. And the bushes in Grandmother Katy Rose's gardens need trimming."

"Wait, Bee," said Mama. Daddy patted her shoulder as if to back up anything she was going to say. "There's no reason Grandfather shouldn't relax a little now that he's retired. He did a magnificent job running the factory for years. And, as we all know, he didn't want the job in the first place. Why can't he be a little easygoing in his old age?" Mama sounded very logical. But Daddy says he's never known Aunt Bee to let logic get in her way.

The Bulldozer rattled her bracelets. "You call it easygoing. I call it heading for his second childhood. If he is not taken in hand, he could disgrace us all. One night, if you can picture it, I saw him sitting on the curb with Robert Junior and Allison as if he were their age. Something must be done."

Uncle Robert never says much when The Bulldozer is carrying on but he asked, "What do you suggest?"

Aunt Bee started to say something. But before the words could escape she clamped her lips over them. Beside me Robby clenched his fists. He whispered, "Listen to her talking against Grandfather." I put my hand over his mouth. I wanted to hear Aunt Bee's plot. She doesn't just sit and talk. She goes into action.

The Bulldozer ran her hands down the front of her yellow dress as if smoothing wrinkles. But there were no wrinkles. She was pausing the way actresses do before they say something important. "My point is, Grandfather is letting the family down. We have a respected place in this town and we each must present a good image. He should, too." Mama sniffed. Nobody cares less about their image than Mama.

"Oh, you scoff, Fran," Aunt Bee went on," but our family has been the heart of Godolphinville ever since Great-grandfather started the furniture factory. It is our duty to set a good example. I have drummed that into Carolina since she was little. Have I not?" She turned to Carolina who sat up straight and put her feet on the floor.

"You certainly have, Mother," Carolina answered. Her tone was so snippy it should have insulted the Bulldozer.

But Aunt Bee was too wound up to listen to anyone but herself. "And while we are talking of duty, I think we must all demand more of Allison. It does the family no credit when she runs through town acting like an undisciplined boy. You must remind her that more is expected of her because she is a Godolphin."

"Now she's plotting against me," I began, but Robby pinched my mouth closed.

All Daddy said was, "We'll see to Allison," but the way he said it made Aunt Bee bite her lip.

"Who will take Grandfather in hand, then?" Aunt Bee's voice was a sort of wail. "It is obvious he is failing rapidly."

"I don't agree that he's failing or needs taking in hand," Mama said. The way her freckles stood out was the only sign she was getting mad.

Uncle Robert said, "He'd hate it if we went over there

cleaning around. His house is just the way he likes it, a little dusty but neat. I think you should stop worrying about him, Beezy." Beezy? Was Uncle Robert making fun of Aunt Bee using that childish nickname? You never can tell with Uncle Robert unless you can see if his eyes are twinkling.

"How can you say the house is neat when there are books everywhere?" We'd heard The Bulldozer rave about Grandfather's books a hundred times. "What must people think when they stop to visit and can't sit down without taking books off the chair? There are even books on the edge of his bathtub."

"And he always wants to read them out loud to you," Carolina said. "It's sooooo boring."

Robby and I forgot about keeping quiet. We jumped up. "Boring!" Robby shouted.

"Grandfather isn't either headed for his second childhood," I shouted, scraping my ear against a lilac branch.

The heads on stage swung toward us all at once, eyes peering out into the darkness. Aunt Bee was first to recover. "So, Allison, now we discover you eavesdropping. You would be punished for this if you were my daughter."

I knew I was likely to be punished even though I wasn't her daughter. Lucky for me, Mama was probably the one who'd do the punishing.

Uncle Robert put an end to the squabble by standing up. "Come on, son," he called to Robby. "It's time to go home. Thanks for the party, Fran." He kissed Mama and grinned at Aunt Bee. "Goodnight all." Stepping off the patio he led

Robby away. Robby looked back, his eyes full of things he wanted to say.

"Go up to your room, Allison," Daddy said, opening the patio door so I could walk through into the house. He didn't sound all that angry.

As I passed Carolina she held out a folded paper. "One last birthday greeting," she said. Aunt Bee smiled around, calling everyone to notice Carolina's generous spirit.

I read her message under the hall light. There was no doubt it came from Carolina. Her generous spirit was all over it:

> Tock tick, tick tock,
> Whose face
> Would stop a clock?
> Allison's, Allison's, Allison's—UGH!

Hurrying into the dining room I picked up Katy Rose's heavy clock and staggered up to my room with it. I didn't feel selfish about it anymore.

Through my window I flashed my flashlight three times. Down R Street three winks of light flicked back from Robby's room. They were followed by Morse code: N-E-E-D T-O T-A-L-K.

I wanted to beam back: Is this is what Shakespeare meant by shallows and miseries? But that was too long. I just sent: C-O-M-E T-O B-R-E-A-K-F-A-S-T. And went to bed.

# 5

## *All Because of Aunt Bee*

I woke up the next morning feeling scared. I'd had a nightmare about being chased and I lay in bed glad to find myself safe. The Allison, Allison, Allison—UGH! chants were giving me bad dreams.

They'd started about a month before our birthday party after Aunt Bee grounded Carolina for getting out of hand. She couldn't even go to the town pool. In the heat of an Illinois summer that was like sending her out on the Sahara desert without her Girl Scout canteen.

Carolina spent her lonely hours writing mean verses about

me. She was mad because I was the one who got her in trouble, though I hadn't meant to.

What happened was, one afternoon Carolina told Aunt Bee she'd be at Melody's practicing cheers. The Consolidated Junior High has a seventh-grade cheerleading squad, and Carolina had decided she and her friends were going to get on it. They practiced all the time.

But somehow, that day, Carolina got sidetracked from her splits and handsprings. And unfortunately Aunt Bee, who was supposed to be at a bridge party, went looking for her. On the way she met me riding my bike. She asked had I seen Carolina. Not knowing anything was going on, I said the last time I saw her she was behind the school gym with Melody and Lisa.

Aunt Bee found them there writing things on the outside of the gym with chalk. But since I'd ridden by, some older boys had arrived. They were trying to erase what the girls wrote and write their own things. The girls were squealing. The boys were pushing and laughing. I guess it looked like they were having too good a time together. Because Aunt Bee treated Carolina as if she'd caught her robbing the Godolphinville Security Bank.

Carolina called me up a couple of days later to pick a fight. "You told where I was on purpose. You knew she'd get mad at me."

"How should I know she was on the warpath?"

Have you ever noticed how people in an argument ignore your questions? That's what Carolina did. She skipped to a different subject. "It's your fault Mother's always after me lately. If you'd start growing up, maybe she'd let me grow up, too. Melody and Lisa can wear teen clothes and jewelry and makeup and stuff and I can't. And you know why? Because everytime I ask her for something like that she says, 'It will be time enough for those kinds of things when Fran lets Allison.'"

"Mama doesn't buy me those things because I don't want them. But she'd talk sense to Aunt Bee about you having them if you asked her. You know she would."

"And if I got grounded for a simple little thing like being with some boys, what do you think she'd do if she found out I talked about her with Aunt Fran? Use your brain."

"Then I'll talk to Mama."

"Don't you dare. That'd be worse than if I did. But do me a favor for once. Stop dressing so sloppy and ask Aunt Fran to buy you some Junior High kind of clothes. And not tomboy ones. You're a mess."

I guess she expected me to say, "Whatever you say, dear cousin." Instead, I was so tired of her bossing me around I said, "I'll be older than Grandfather before I want to look like Melody and Lisa Pierce."

"You shouldn't have said that."

"I'd like to know why not."

"Because until you start acting your age so Mother lets me start acting mine, I'm going to make you sorry you were ever born." She slammed down the phone.

I was hot all over and had started to go for a drink when

the phone rang again. It was Carolina. She didn't even say hello or who she was. "I suppose you're going to tattle to Aunt Fran and Uncle Peter about what I said."

"Have I ever?" I asked her.

She must have been trying to remember a time she could accuse me of because it took her awhile to say, "No, but there's always a first time."

"Well, this won't be it," I said. And she slammed the phone down again.

I thought that was the end of the fight and was glad it was over. Usually Carolina and I don't get mad. We just ignore each other. She has her friends and I have mine. But it turned out the phone calls were only the beginning.

After she got free of her grounding, the chants started. She added the mean verses she'd made up about me to their cheerleading routines. It seemed as if everywhere I went, Melody and Lisa Pierce and Carolina were there waiting. They even whispered the chants at me over the back of the seats during the Saturday movie at The Purple Plaza. But they were sneaky. If adults were listening, they didn't do it.

I'd gotten really tired of hearing things like:

> "Allison, Allison, Allison Cox
> Wrap her and strap her
> And shove her in a box,
> Allison, Allison, Allison—UGH!"

And while they chanted, the three of them did exactly the same bends and kicks and wiggles. Robby tried to get me to tell Mama or Grandfather. But he knew I couldn't. Especially since I'd promised Carolina I wouldn't. And anyway, tattling is one of the few things Mama punishes for.

I lay in my bed thinking about the teasing for the hundreth time. I wished I knew how to stop it other than doing what Carolina wanted. Now that school was going to start pretty soon and the teasing might follow me to Luxor, I'd begun to worry.

Mama called up the stairs to say breakfast was ready. While I dressed I heard her down there halfheartedly scolding Robby. I suppose she was so stirred up by her argument the night before with Aunt Bee that she didn't have many bad feelings left for us. She was busy serving breakfast when I got downstairs and forgot to mention the evils of eavesdropping.

Breakfast at our house is serious business. Robby likes to come for it because he and Uncle Robert only eat cornflakes. He says the trouble with cornflakes is they have no breakfast smell. Mama's meals in the morning smell up our whole house. Whiffs of coffee mingle together with eggs frying in bacon grease and rolls baking. It makes getting out of bed worthwhile.

Mama says a hot breakfast makes a difference in the way the day turns out. We're supposed to give it our full attention, eat slowly, and carry on an intelligent conversation.

Daddy's idea of an intelligent conversation that morning was to give Robby and me a message from the sheriff. "Joe Watson called and asked you two to put your flashlights away."

"How come?" Robby asked. "He already made us put them away all of July."

"Someone woke him last night phoning to report burglars flashing around in one of our upstairs rooms."

"Not again!" I was disgusted. "It's probably that man renting the house on the corner. He hasn't lived in Godolphinville long enough to know there aren't any burglars."

"He probably hasn't," Mama said. "But that's no reason for you to convince him there are."

"If we can't use our flashlights," Robby said, "we'll forget all that Morse code it took us so long to learn."

"I guess you'll just have to forget it, then," Daddy said. "He also wanted to know if you two had been doing any target practice on the side of the library."

"With what?"

"Tomatoes. Somebody's been throwing them and he hasn't been able to catch whoever it is. They're making a mess. Is it you, Robby?"

"Not me, Uncle Peter."

"Allison?"

"No, Daddy. That sounds like little kids."

"I'm glad it wasn't either of you. I thought it sounded like little kids, too."

Usually Robby and I take our time over breakfast. But that morning we wanted to get through and talk over what Aunt Bee said about Grandfather. Daddy slowed us up by putting more omelet and sausage on our plates. Mama kept refilling our glasses with milk and orange juice. At last Robby couldn't stand hanging around any longer. He asked to be excused without even eating a sweet roll.

That worried Mama. Since his mother left to be an artist in New York she's mothered Robby as much as she mothers me. "Are you feeling all right, Robby?"

"I feel fine, Aunt Fran."

"You didn't eat a roll. You usually eat two."

"Or three," Daddy said. He was buttering his fourth.

Robby reached over and took a caramel bun in each hand. "May I take these with me?"

Mama tucked a paper napkin in his pocket. "It's only a little past seven-thirty. Surely you can't have a soccer game this early."

"No. But I have serious things to talk over with Allison. Come on, Al, let's go."

Daddy sent me the kind of look across the table that means trouble. "You sit back down, Robby. I have serious things to talk over with Allison first. Drink your juice, Allison, and come into my study." I should have known I wouldn't escape without a talking-to.

"How many times," he began as soon as I closed the door, "have I told you it's impolite to listen in on private conversations?"

I knew he didn't want an exact count so I just shrugged. "It didn't seem like a private conversation to me. Aunt Bee was talking in her loudest voice out on the patio. Anybody could have overheard her."

For a second he looked ready to laugh. Instead he took a deep breath and straightened his shoulders. That's the trouble with grownups. They stick together against kids even when they're mad at each other. "You know you're not to listen to what people say unless they know you're hearing. You didn't think about that last night, did you?"

"No." Though I didn't feel I'd done wrong, I knew I'd get an easier punishment if I agreed with him.

"I planned to give you a break this year. I wasn't going to make you wear Bee's birthday present to the reunion. But she's right about one thing. You shouldn't have been listening in without announcing you were out there in the dark. So you'll just have to suffer through wearing that elaborate pink creation with all its lace and ribbons. And while you have it on, remember why."

I groaned. It hadn't occurred to me I could ever, ever escape those twin dresses. Now here was Daddy mentioning that it was possible and snatching it away at the same time. But I didn't argue. When he's disciplining he doesn't want backtalk. If I try to make a point in my favor, he adds another terrible twist to my punishment. He'd be sending me to the Snappy Scissors Beauty Salon to have my hair permed for the reunion if I didn't shut up.

I turned to leave. As I opened the door he said, "You

know I'm doing this for your own good." But I didn't know that at all. He was doing it out of duty to Aunt Bee and that made me mad.

When I marched out of the study I must have looked really angry. Mama squeezed my hand as I brushed by the table and Robby asked, "Did he beat you?"

I stamped ahead of him down the hall. "You know he never hits me."

"What did he say?"

"I'm too mad to talk about it. Okay?"

"Okay."

I slammed open the screen door and went out and threw myself down on the grass under the crab apple tree. It was already hot. Cars buzzed past headed for the factory, blowing dust up behind them. Across Front Street Mrs. Pierce was sweeping her walk. Her collie slipped past her and ran into the street chasing a faded green Volkswagen, growling and biting its tires. Mrs. Pierce hurried along the sidewalk after him, her broom raised as if she was going to shoot.

When the car outraced him, Whiskey came prancing back all excited. Mrs. Pierce banged him with her broom and he ran behind the house whining, his proud tail between his legs. After my talk with Daddy I knew just how that poor dog felt. The whole day was off to a bad start in spite of Mama's hot breakfast.

# 6

## Robby Gives Me
## Something Unexpected

Robby chewed his second caramel bun and watched me snatch heads off dandelions. He began picking a long stemmed one each time I beheaded one. He'd hold it in front of his face, cross his eyes and say, "Who elected you boss of the whole family, Aunt Bee?" Then he'd make a horrible face at the flower before he threw it into the street. Soon I was laughing.

I forgot Daddy's punishment and thought about what The Bulldozer'd said the night before. "I want to find out what Aunt Bee is planning to do, Robby. We know she thinks Grandfather is going to disgrace the family. But we don't know how she expects to stop him."

"The Bulldozer, you mean." He began licking the sticky stuff from the caramel bun off his hands but stopped when he ran into some dandelion juice.

"Yeah, The Bulldozer. When she starts to work on somebody, they better watch out."

"At least you know she's after you, Al. But poor Grandfather doesn't. Why don't we walk over and warn him?" He got up but I waved him down.

"You don't just go up to a father and blab about his daughter."

"The Bulldozer isn't very daughterly. She's more like a crab apple with a worm in it down somebody's back." He dropped one down mine. I guess the way I screeched showed him I understood what he meant. He asked, "So how do we stop her?"

We thought about his question. He didn't come up with an answer. Neither did I. We sat there sorting through the grass for four-leaf clovers but didn't find any. At last I said, "What about the quote Grandfather taught us? He said there was wisdom in it."

Robby repeated the first two lines:

" 'There is a tide in the affairs of men
    Which, taken at the flood, leads on to fortune'

45

Don't tell Grandfather, but to me that's just a lot of words strung together. Maybe he was right about there being wisdom in it, but I'm not wise to it." When I didn't laugh he bumped me with his elbow. "I'm not wise to wisdom. Get it?"

"I got it, haha. But this is no time to fool around. Be serious. Grandfather said part of it meant when it's time to begin something, don't hang back."

"Okay. But what shall we begin to do?"

"Protect Grandfather from Aunt Bee."

"How?"

I looked for a fingernail to chew on to help me think. They hadn't grown much since the last time I'd needed one to bite. But there was enough nail to give me one idea. "We could try brainstorming."

"What's that?"

"A special way to solve a problem. My sixth-grade teacher taught us how to do it. You put everybody's ideas in the same pot, stir them, and come out with an answer. There's one rule: Any idea counts. Want to try it?"

"Sure."

"You start."

He rubbed his hands and grinned. "I've got a good one. We run away and take Grandfather with us."

"That's dumb!"

"You said any idea counts."

"I didn't mean crazy ones."

I'd hurt his feelings. He dug in the dirt with his finger and didn't look up. I said, "I meant like how about me going through his closet, finding the shirts with buttons missing and sewing them on?"

"You can't sew." He was sulking.

"I know. But I guess just about anybody can do buttons."

"I suppose I could hide his slippers so he'd have to wear his shoes," he said slowly.

"Perfect! But there's one more thing. Remember Uncle Robert asking The Bulldozer, 'What do you suggest?' The Bulldozer started to say something and then stopped. I think she's got stuff planned that she's not telling. We need to find out what it is."

"You don't want to brainstorm that, too? Let's do something fun for a while."

"We'll just work on this one thing, Robby. Then we'll find somebody to play with." I'd show him some smart thinking. "Maybe she's planning to send Grandfather to a nursing home."

"That's stupid. He'd never go. And our parents would never let him, either." Robby stood on his head. He's not good at it. He had to do a lot of kicking to keep balanced.

I tried again. "Maybe she's planning to take Grandfather to live with her. So she can keep him looking neat and acting proper."

Robby fell over, his face red from hanging upside down. "That's even more stupid than your first idea. You know their place is too small for three people."

"How can we brainstorm if every time I say something,

you say it's stupid?" Now I was digging in the dirt. We sat silent a long time. Then I said, "All I know is she's out to get Grandfather. And if I tell Mama and Daddy they won't really listen because it's August. And Uncle Robert won't have time to think about it. And if we tell Grandfather he'll say, 'Whatever's best for the family.'"

"How do you know he'll say that?"

"Because he always puts the family ahead of himself. Just the way he gave up being a professor to run Great-grandfather's factory when there wasn't anybody else to do it. Just the way he gave Carolina and me Katy Rose's portrait and clock. They're his favorite things but he wants us to learn something from having them. So it's just you and me left to stop Aunt Bee. We've got to be strong and forceful and fight, fight, fight."

"You sound just like The Bulldozer."

I couldn't believe he'd said that. "Robby Godolphin, that's the meanest thing you ever said in your whole life. I hate you." And to let him know I meant it, I yanked his hair.

Next thing I knew we were rolling around on the ground hitting and yelling. I would have bitten him if I'd gotten a chance. But Robby is fast and tricky. Suddenly blood spurted out of his nose. Robby, my friend, my favorite person in all the world. I pulled back and Robby, my friend, my favorite person in all the world, landed his fist right in my eye.

Lights flashed in my head and my eardrums twanged. The

side of my face hurt worse than if it had been whacked with a board. I looked at Robby with my one good eye. His mouth hung open. But he closed it pretty quick because of the blood running in. "I'm sorry," he mumbled.

"Hang your head down and bleed into the street so you won't get it all over. I'll get a wet towel." Before I could stagger up, a car stopped and Aunt Bee put her head out the window. Carolina leaned forward in the seat beside her.

"Why is your head in the gutter, Robert Junior?" asked The Bulldozer. "You could be struck by a passing car."

"I have a nosebleed." His voice was all muffled.

Looking at me she asked, "What is the matter with your eye?"

I wasn't going to lie and set myself up for another of Daddy's punishments. So I asked, "Can you tell if I might be getting a sty?"

She studied the eye. I was glad she didn't get out of her car and come closer. "Not a sty. That would be in just one spot. Has your mother seen it?"

"No, it just started."

"It looks awful and so do you," said Carolina, adding her two bits. She had on a big smile. "Did Robby hit you Allison, Allison?"

"Don't try to be funny," I said, scared by how true her guess was.

"I must say, excitement follows you two around like a pet dog," Aunt Bee said. "I shudder to think what the neighbors are making of your antics this morning. Go on inside. Put some ice on Robert's nose and ask your mother to take care of your eye." She drove off shaking her head.

Robby's nose stopped pouring blood. "Let's go wash. If Mama and Daddy are still reading the newspapers on the patio, we won't have to explain."

We were in luck. As we tiptoed down the hall we could see them through the dining room window. Daddy was doing the crossword puzzle. Mama had the sports page. They didn't know we'd come in.

We got the blood off Robby except where he'd wiped his hands on his white shorts. When we finished he looked straight at me for the first time. He blinked and looked again. "I think I gave you a black eye. It's already turning blue. No wonder. Look." He held out his hand. He had on an old ring of Uncle Robert's he wears sometimes. So that was why it hurt so much when he hit me.

I looked in the mirror over the sink and touched around my face. Pain shot through it. All I could think of was going to the reunion with a black eye. If it lasted that long it was going to look especially gruesome above that fancy pink dress.

# 7

## *Trouble and More Trouble*

**B**ecause Robby's nose might start bleeding again and because of my eye, we gave up trying to save Grandfather from Aunt Bee that day. We played cards on the cool cement floor of the garage until Mama called us in for lunch.

When she saw my eye she hustled me into the car and took me over to Dr. Sedgwick. He said there wasn't much he could do. It was going to be a doozer of a bruised eye because of Robby's ring. Mama said there had to be something that would help. So he said she could put on wet packs if she wanted. "I'm afraid you're going to be starting school with a black eye no matter what your mother does," he told me.

When we got home Mama sent me up to bed. She brought me a chicken sandwich and chocolate milk on a tray. And Daddy came upstairs to hang Katy Rose's clock on my wall. He pulled the chains so the pendulum would start swinging and the loud ticks would keep me company.

All afternoon Mama kept putting dry hot packs and cold wet packs on my eye. She thought that would take the color out. But when I looked in the mirror that night I saw that the packs had acted like sunshine and rain on one of Daddy's rosebushes. My eye was really beginning to bloom.

I fell asleep with a tight feeling across the right side of my head. All through the night the bonging of the clock kept waking me up. "What does Grandfather want me to learn from you?" I whispered into the dark. The swish, swish, swish of the pendulum was all the answer I got.

The next day Robby and I went over to get to work improving Grandfather. We found him at his desk. He's used to us running in and out, so he just gave us each an absentminded kiss and went on writing letters.

Robby meant to start by hiding Grandfather's slippers. But Grandfather had them on. We didn't know it then but everything we tried to do that day was going to turn out wrong.

We went into the hall to consult. "You can come over later and hide his slippers," I whispered. "Why don't you go see if shingles really are gone off the roof. Maybe The Bulldozer just added that to make it sound worse. I'll go sort through his shirts."

"We better hurry. She could be on her way over here to start in on him herself."

Grandfather's closet smelled good from the pomander I make him every Christmas by sticking cloves all over an orange. His shirts hung neatly on hangers. His ties lay smoothed out on a special rack. I wished I could phone Aunt Bee and say, "You were dead wrong about him being messy. Come see how tidy he is." But that would have given away what we were doing.

Five shirts had missing buttons. I looked around on top of his dresser to see if he'd kept the ones that fell off. He had a little china tray with "Souvenir of Mackinac Island" painted on it in silver letters but no buttons. There were only pennies and paper clips and one old-fashioned gold collar stud that he doesn't use anymore. I didn't dare open his drawers and search there. Mama would have grounded me forever.

Robby surprised me by sliding silently into the room. He must have tiptoed upstairs, stepping around the places that creak. He'd snagged the threads of his T-shirt and his legs had fresh scrapes on top of the old ones. "I couldn't see the roof from the ground so I shinnied up the tree by the porch. Even from there I couldn't see the roof. I don't know how Aunt Bee did unless she flew over it on her broom." I bet he'd been practicing that last line all the way from the top of the tree.

I handed him the rack of ties. "I'm going home for a needle and thread. You take these to the Cleanerama and get them cleaned. Charge them to Grandfather. If he doesn't have an account there, charge them to Daddy."

"Why not charge them to The Bulldozer? She's the only one who cares that they're spotty."

"Yes, but she's also the only one who'd care about having to pay the bill." We went down the front stairs together, hanging over the railing, watching for Grandfather. We didn't want him asking us any questions.

I ran home for Mama's sewing box and took it back to Grandfather's bedroom. I started sewing buttons on his brown striped shirt because it's the one he likes the most.

I still think I was right when I told Robby just about anybody can sew on buttons. But I turned out to be different. In Mama's box there were plenty of those little white ones men fasten their shirts with. But they didn't take to being sewed on. I'd stick in the needle and, flip, the button would hop away like we were playing some game. So I gave up on those and chose a big one that was easier to hold onto. While I sewed, the thread kept tying itself in knots down under the shirt. I knew right then I'd hate Home Ec. if I had to take it in Junior High.

It seemed Robby had just left when he came back, not saying anything, looking at the wall as if he had no idea I was there. He seemed paler than usual but he had so much chocolate around his mouth I couldn't be sure. He pulled the tie rack from behind his back and held it in my face. Grandfather's ties looked as if they'd exploded. "I did just what you said. I washed them and dried them and look at them!" I'd never heard him sound like such a loser.

"Robby, I didn't say get them clean. I said get them cleaned. Clean-E-D. Dry-cleaned."

"Oh." He sat down on Grandfather's bed with his back to me and put his head on his knees. The rack of destroyed ties lay beside him. The Cleanerama machines that the ads say are UTTERLY DEPENDABLE had blasted Grandfather's beautiful Christmas and birthday ties to rags. It was the worst thing we'd ever done. But Robby, hunched down, looked as destroyed as the ties, so I didn't say so.

"I'm not having any luck with the buttons, either." I shook out the brown striped shirt and held it up. Grandfather wouldn't even be able to get into it. I'd sewed the collar and the back together. "Give me those ties."

Robby raised his head. "What're you going to do?"

"Put the ties and this mean shirt in the trash. What else can I do? You hang these others back in his closet behind something. Maybe then he'll think he's out of shirts and go buy some new ones." I felt like storming around but didn't want Grandfather to hear me and come to see what was going on.

"What about the ties? We'll really get it in our fortune

55

cookies if we don't do something quick. I ruined every one he owned unless he had one on this morning. Did he?"

I pictured Grandfather at his desk. He'd had on his brown house sweater, full of holes. He likes it best and keeps wearing it, even though people give him new ones hoping he'll throw the old one away. Under it he had a wool shirt. And I'd seen his underwear where his shirt collar was unbuttoned. Even in August when the heat in Godolphinville is too much for everybody else, he's cold. "No, he didn't have one on."

"Then what shall we do?"

"I don't know yet." The thought of the ties made me want to throw up, but it wouldn't help to say so. "I'll have to think about the tie problem later."

"Brainstorm it?" Robby's nice but he can needle you as bad as anybody when he's in a down mood.

"Just go on. Put the shirts back. I'll get his hammer. We'll nail that board Aunt Bee was complaining about back on the fence."

We were better at the board. It still had the nails in it, though they were rusty and bent. All it needed was a couple of smacks.

Then we started trimming bushes. I think the tie disaster had made Robby doubt he could do anything right. He said, "Let's practice behind the house where they don't show." He set to work. The old garden shears creaked as he opened them and ground their teeth as he closed them. He grunted a lot. I told him where to clip.

"Over there on the left. My left, your right. No, that's too much. OOPS."

Robby shoved the clippers at me. "You do it if you know so much." He stalked right out of the garden and down the street, not even looking back to see if I was sorry. He'd stopped just in time. The bush was about gone.

I was glad he'd given me the shears. The whole time he'd been trimming I'd been sure there was a better way to do it. I moved around the corner to another row of bushes and set to work. Grunt, squeak, clip, oh no, squeak, clip.

"Allison, why are you cutting up my blueberry bush?" Grandfather had come up behind me, quiet in his soft slippers. His voice was angry.

"I thought it needed trimming," I said with my fingers crossed. It was The Bulldozer who thought it needed trimming.

"You're ruining my bush, child. You've cut out the heart where the berries would have come next summer. Whatever were you thinking of?" Grandfather started gathering up the clipped branches.

"Grandfather, I'm sorry. I was trying to help you and instead I'm messing everything up." I threw the clippers as hard as I could. They hit the fence, and the board we just nailed on fell off with a crash.

"I don't want any help. Especially if you're going to throw things. My bushes are just the way I want them." He looked around at his careless jungle of a garden.

It's a dangerous way for them to be, I thought, but I

didn't say anything. As I told Robby, you can't go around blabbing to fathers about their daughters.

Then Grandfather noticed my eye. He dropped the branches and laid his hands on each side of my face. They felt cool and dry, and my anger seeped away. His must have, too, because he asked kindly, "Do you want to tell me what happened?"

"No, thank you. Maybe some other time."

"Then come inside. You can rest your eyes while I read." We went in and I chose a book off the shelf where Grandfather puts things he thinks Robby and I will be interested in. He read to me about ants and how they have little farms inside their hills. After about four pages I began to feel sleepy. I knew it wouldn't matter if I took a nap. Grandfather begins reading aloud and then forgets you're there. Usually that treatment makes everything seem better. But when I woke up, nothing was any better than it had been that morning. In fact, considering the ties, and the shirt I'd ruined, and Robby being mad, things were much worse.

When Grandfather arrived at our house for supper with the family on Sunday, he had on his shoes but no tie. It was probably the first time since he started wearing them that he'd been out in public without one. My heart dropped when I saw him. I'd forgotten about solving the tie problem.

Mama hugged him. "You're looking sporty tonight. I'm glad you came without a tie in this heat. This kind of day makes me wonder why Americans don't wear sarongs like people in Malaysia."

"It's an odd thing," Grandfather told her. "When I went up to dress I couldn't find my slippers, my favorite striped shirt, or a single tie."

You can always tell when Aunt Bee thinks she's been proved right. It's something about her eyebrows. They say "I told you so," even though she doesn't come right out and say it herself. She sang softly while she put the fruit salad on the table. Her eyebrows kept looking pleased clear through supper to the homemade peach ice cream.

After we'd eaten Robby pulled me into Daddy's study. "I don't know what William Shakespeare was talking about, do you? When it was time to start working against Aunt Bee we didn't hang back and all it's brought us is trouble."

"That's not the worst part. All it's brought Grandfather is trouble, too. Now The Bulldozer is absolutely certain he's losing his mind. Whoever heard of anyone not being able to find their slippers and shirt and ties right in their very own closet?"

So far the birthday present that had turned out the worst was the Shakespeare quote from Grandfather.

# 8

## Advice and a Warning

Robby walked into our dining room the next day while we were eating cold tuna chowder and summer apples. He had a brown paper bag and a hungry look. Mama asked him if he had time to eat with us just as if we didn't know that was what he'd come hoping for. He said, "Yes, thank you, Aunt Fran," and went and got a bowl and began filling it up.

"What's in your bag?" Daddy asked him.

"Something for Allison."

"Shall I try to guess what it is?" Daddy likes having Robby around to joke with. Sometimes their conversations sound like friendly wrestling matches. But Robby didn't seem to be in a wrestling mood.

"It's just some old books."

After lunch we went up to my room and I was upset to find what the old books were. Robby had taken two volumes out of Grandfather's Sherlock Holmes collection. "But Robby, these are worth a lot of money. Grandfather will never speak to us again if anything happens to them."

"Nothing's going to happen to them."

"Why did you take them?"

"To study how the greatest detective in history picked up clues, Al. We aren't getting anywhere finding out what The Bulldozer's up to. This might help with that."

"You mean if we study Sherlock's style and Aunt Bee's style maybe we can figure out what she plans to do to Grandfather? Like brainstorming, huh?" I couldn't help making that dig at Robby, he'd been such a pig. "Anyway, it's worth a try. I've had an idea, too. Do you have any money?"

"About four dollars. And Pip owes me some. Why?"

"The ties."

"We'll never have enough to replace those ties."

"No, but we have to do something. When he goes out without one it's like he has half his clothes off. We won't try to replace them all, just two or three. Because with ties he does the same as with his brown sweater. He wears some over and over and doesn't wear the others at all."

"Yeah, you're right."

"So we'll pool our money, buy him as many as we can, and sneak them into his closet." Robby took my money and left to take care of the ties. He'd already taken care of them once. I hoped he'd do better the second time.

I started on the Sherlock Holmes book, but Daddy let out a yelp downstairs. "Allison, come help me. The Pierces' collie is in our yard. One sweep of his tail will finish my daylilies."

I went down and we rounded up Whiskey. Daddy slid a rope through the dog collar and held it out to me. "Why don't you take him home?"

I wasn't anxious to, in case I ran into Lisa. But I couldn't explain that without explaining a lot of other things, so I went.

Across the street I could see Mrs. Pierce sitting behind the trumpet vine that grows up their porch. She was rocking and talking to the preacher we met under the mulberry tree. She goes to his Church of the Baptismal Fire but the rest of her family hasn't taken it up yet.

When I got closer I could hear ice clinking in glasses. I knew they must be drinking water or lemonade. The Baptismal Fire people think tea and coffee and soft drinks are sinful.

"Mrs. Pierce," I called. "Whiskey was in our yard. I've brought him home."

She came to the top of her steps. "Whiskers," she said.

"Excuse me?" What was she talking about?

"I wish you wouldn't call our collie that dreadful name, Allison. His name is Whiskers."

Whiskers? I remember the day they got him. Mr. Pierce and his brother were playing horseshoes in the yard. They were drinking out of fat little glasses and shouting when they scored a point. Their horseshoes rang against the iron stake. When Lisa showed them her new puppy they each tipped a drop out of their glasses on the dog's little head. Mr. Pierce said, "I hereby name thee Whiskey."

Yet there stood Mrs. Pierce naming the dog over again. It wasn't nearly as special as the first time. She turned and called into the house, "Lisa, come get your dog." But Lisa didn't appear.

"Well, here he is anyhow," I said, glad not to meet Lisa face to face. I wrapped the rope around the rail of the steps and started down the walk.

But Reverend Kean said, "Come up. Come up. We will extend our prayer circle." His voice was so deep his words seemed to drop down and roll along the porch floor.

I wanted to get back to Sherlock Holmes but didn't see how I could politely refuse to stay. I went up on the porch. Whiskey pulled loose and followed me and stretched himself out by the preacher's feet.

Mrs. Pierce called in through the screen door, "Lisa, you and Carolina put that game away. Come on out here and bring a glass of ice water for Allison."

Oh, squash, I thought, Carolina and Lisa both! In a few minutes they came out, glaring at me as if it was my fault they'd had to give up their game. The game they were playing must have been called Snappy Scissors Beauty Salon because they both had on eye makeup and green nail polish. Lisa was in her best dress for the preacher's visit. She looked hot and uncomfortable. So I wasn't surprised when she drank the glass of water instead of passing it to me.

"Let us join together in a prayer for rain," Reverend Kean said. "The farms are suffering for lack of it. The corn is as dry as a neighbor who's been out in the hot sun without a glass of water." He didn't look at Lisa but she blushed anyway. "So, young ladies—" He looked at me, then, and cleared his throat. "You are a young lady, aren't you?"

I suppose it wasn't easy to tell, me in my jean shorts and T-shirt that said "Indy 500—Zooooooooooom" and bare feet and my hair cut short because of all the cowlicks in it that whirl in different directions. But I wished he hadn't asked me right out like that. I knew Carolina was glad everybody stood staring at me, seeing what a tomboy I was. "Yes, sir, I am." Mama always makes me say "Sir" to our minister.

"She's Allison Cox from across the street, Reverend Kean," Mrs. Pierce said.

"Then we've met before, the other night when you were out walking with your grandfather."

"Yes, sir." He seemed to tangle me up in words. Would I ever get back to Sherlock Holmes?

"I met your grandfather again at the drug store and he joined me in prayer." I could picture my dignified grandfather and this excitable preacher bowing their heads beside the table of perfumed soaps. The druggist tells everybody the town news. How he must have gossipped about that!

Carolina spoke for the first time. "He's my grandfather, too." I suppose she thought I was trying to claim Grandfather all for myself.

"Shall we begin?" Reverend Kean asked. This praying in stores and on porches wasn't something Carolina and I were used to. Our minister saves it for church. But if Grandfather thought it was all right, so did I. The preacher held out his hand and I took it. Lisa and Carolina stood stiff as corn stalks.

"Each one in the prayer circle increases the power," the preacher said. He took Lisa's hand. She frowned. Carolina stared through the trumpet vine, her hands behind her back. Mrs. Pierce took my other hand.

Reverend Kean addressed his Maker in a friendly voice. He told Him how to save the Godolphinville farms from drying up. He prayed for a long time as if he thought God was very hard to convince. He told Him about wind and clouds and rain and hail and thermals and sunlight and shadow. I think he even mentioned continental drift, though I don't see how that fitted in. Maybe my mind wandered. It was like a sermon, with Reverend Kean in the pulpit and God the only person in the church. He finished with a loud Amen that swayed the leaves on the trumpet vine.

It swayed everybody in the prayer circle, too. Lisa and Carolina shot into the house. I said goodbye to the preacher. As we shook hands he pulled me down and whispered, "Watch out for tomatoes." I'd have thought I'd misunderstood him except he speaks so clearly. Watch out for tomatoes? Whiskey named Whiskers? Everybody was talking crazy that afternoon. But I thanked him and ran home. I had two questions I needed to ask Daddy.

He was eating a sandwich in the kitchen with the radio on announcing a baseball game. In the living room he had the TV turned to a different game. He strolled back and forth between them dropping crumbs.

I told Daddy about Mrs. Pierce renaming her dog right there in front of Reverend Kean. It seemed to me that was a kind of lie. But Daddy seemed very interested. He said, "That's the first time I ever heard of a dog with an undercover name."

He hadn't gotten the point at all. Mrs. Pierce was afraid of what Reverend Kean would think of Whiskey's name. It was just like The Bulldozer being afraid of what people would think of Grandfather. And of me. Was every lady in town, except Mama, afraid of what other people would think?

"Reverend Kean looked at me funny because he couldn't tell right off whether I was a boy or a girl. Aunt Bee and Carolina think it's awful I'm a tomboy. Does it matter?"

"It doesn't matter to me," Daddy said giving me a hug. He took another bite of his sandwich and a slice of cucumber shot out covered with mayonnaise. It landed on the rug. Daddy didn't notice because just then the runner on TV stole a base.

"But should it matter to me? That's what I need to know."

"Why would it?"

"I'm all mixed up about things, Daddy. Some girls in my class have been dressing ladylike all year. Not like this." Looking down at my clothes I could see they weren't even very clean.

"Which way feels more comfortable to you, Allison?"

"This way."

"Then you aren't ready yet. You'll know when it's your time."

"But what if I don't, Daddy? What if I'm still a tomboy when I'm grown?"

"Then that will be your way. But I suspect you'll change. Your mother did." I could tell I was interrupting his game. He was watching TV over my shoulder. But I had to know.

"Mama was a tomboy?"

"The worst kind." Daddy grinned. "She beat up every boy in her class. I was glad I was two years older, too big for her to start in on."

"Mama?" I couldn't picture it. My nice Mama beating up boys. "When did she change?"

"I don't remember exactly. But suddenly there she was

dazzling all the boys in town. I'd climb a ladder and sit in the tree and talk to her through her window when everyone was asleep." He'd forgotten the game.

"Daddy! Didn't Grandfather and Katy Rose find out?"

"If they did, they didn't say so. But I'm not going to be so easy on you, Allison. You're the only daughter I have. When you start bursting into beauty, I'm going to hide our ladder."

"You're silly," I said. But he made me feel better. He wasn't ashamed of me being a tomboy even though Carolina was. I didn't know how I'd know when it was time to start changing my image. Still, it was comforting that Daddy didn't care either way.

I spent the rest of the afternoon with Sherlock Holmes. I read his stories, studying his detective techniques. All the time half my mind was on a question I'd wanted to ask Daddy but couldn't think how to. When he said Mama was dazzling all the boys, what about her nose? Didn't they see it? Didn't she care?

Before I fell asleep that night I read some more. By the time I turned off my flashlight and stuffed the book under my pillow, I felt ready to solve the case of Aunt Bee versus Grandfather. But the case of my nose, I had no answers for.

# 9

## *Suspicions and Clues*

Robby and I began spying around. When nothing turned up, Robby got tired of the detective game and spent most of his time playing with his friends. I kept looking for clues.

I found the first one the afternoon Carolina came calling on Grandfather. She hardly ever came over there. Partly that was because Aunt Bee hired someone to be home with her when school was out. Partly it was because Grandfather wasn't as easy with Carolina as he was with us, though he loved her just as much. He thought he had to amuse her.

He'd sit her down and read to her, expecting her to like that as much as we do. But he was wrong. Carolina isn't into hearing stories any more than she's into tomboys.

So it was a surprise to have her walk in when Grandfather was reading us a book by Altsheler about the American frontier. "Hello, Grandfather," she said. She blew him a kiss. Does she do that to get out of actually kissing him? She gets out of speaking to Robby and me by acting like we aren't there.

Grandfather looked pleased to see her. "My dear child, come join us." He lifted some books off the rocker so she could sit down. "Pass Carolina the cookies, Robby."

After he took a handful, Robby handed Carolina the plate of gingersnaps that always sits on Grandfather's desk. She stared at it before she made up her mind to take one. She worked it out from underneath. I suppose she was avoiding the dust, though with gingersnaps a little doesn't change the flavor. She wiped the cookie on her cutoffs before she broke it and popped it between her perfect teeth.

Grandfather was reading the part where Henry Ware attacks the British gun scows. Robby leaned forward, following every word even though he hears the story often because Grandfather reads it to us and forgets. And then reads it again. The way he does it, I can see everything that's happening. I'm right there, taking part in the action.

Henry Ware and I were hiding in the river. Except for some Indian scouts guarding against frontiersmen like

Henry and me, the tribe was all asleep. Henry and I were getting ready to send the canoe among the enemy boats and blow them up. We had just lighted the gunpowder when Carolina asked, "Isn't that a boy's book, Grandfather?"

It made Robby mad, having her interrupt just before the Indian scouts noticed what Henry Ware was doing. "There aren't boys' books and girls' books, Stupid."

"You're stupid yourself, Robby." Carolina sat back. And Grandfather, who wouldn't miss a word if the Godolphinville Volunteer Fire Fighters ran a practice drill through his house, read right on.

Pretty soon Carolina began scratching here and there as though mosquitoes were after her. She yawned. She said, "Grandfather, may I borrow two dollars?"

As he read, Grandfather put his hand in his side pocket and felt around. He took the book in his other hand so he could feel in the opposite pocket. But he stopped the story only long enough to say, "I have no money with me. Look on my bedside table."

Carolina scuffled out of the room. As Grandfather read about the success of the daring surprise attack, I could hear her upstairs. Doors opened and closed. Drawers slammed in the different bedrooms. She was up there a lot longer than two dollars' worth. Then she ran down the stairs and out the door without a goodbye or a thank you. There's a clue in the way she acted today, I told myself, though I didn't have any idea what it was.

That visit should have been the end of Carolina for a while. But she kept dropping in, poking around. And Aunt Bee came. She wasn't in the habit of visiting Grandfather much oftener than Carolina. I guess she was satisfied just seeing him at the Sunday family suppers.

One night I took some dessert over to Grandfather. We were starting on it when Aunt Bee dropped by. "Join us in some raspberry shortcake," Grandfather said. "Fran sent it over."

"No, thank you. I've just come to see how you are."

"Allison, why don't you make some tea?" Grandfather asked.

I made tea the way Mama showed me, hot for Grandfather, iced for The Bulldozer and me. Then I set a tray with milk and lemon and honey and carried it to the library. I expected to find The Bulldozer lecturing Grandfather about his clothes. But she wasn't there. I found her taking measuring steps around the dining room. She jerked when I said, "It's ready."

We went back in the library and drank our tea. There was a nervous feeling in the air. It wasn't in what we were saying to each other but it was there somewhere, behind the words. I couldn't even tell who felt nervous, so I went home feeling creepy. Was that another clue?

If I'd noticed Aunt Bee's car out in front of Grandfather's house the next night, I probably wouldn't have gone in. But I cut through the back of his garden so I didn't know she was in the house. I let myself into the kitchen and went looking for Grandfather. The door to the library was closed and I could hear talking inside. He never closes the door. What was going on?

Then I heard giggles and whispering from the front hall. I walked around to see who that was. As I stepped into view, everything stopped like I'd pulled out the cord that ran the sound and motion. The gigglers, Carolina and Melody, stood stiff as statues on the stairs, looking guilty.

"What are you doing here?" Carolina asked. She twisted the you. It made her sound very annoyed that I'd turned up.

"I came to take a walk with Grandfather," I said. "What are you here for, Caro?"

"Don't call me Caro," she said, even though all her friends do.

"So why'd you come over here?" I asked again.

"To tell Grandfather good night." That was a fake. She never does that. But her prissy look would've fooled most people.

"I suppose Melody did, too?"

Melody whispered to Carolina. Then she hurried down the stairs and outside. I'd caught them at something. Otherwise they'd have started the Allison, Allison, Allison— UGH! chant right there on Grandfather's curvy front stairs. Carolina and I were left alone, our talk echoing loudly in the hall.

"Why start to play here all of a sudden?" I asked.

"I have as much right to play here as you and Robby do. And I'll bring Melody whenever I want to. Grandfather doesn't belong to you, Nosy."

Nosy? For a minute I thought she was talking about my nose. Could she see it had started growing? I almost reached up to feel it. Then I realized she meant snoopy. "You've never liked it here with Grandfather. You just come when you want something from him."

"Why don't you tell that to Grandfather so he'll put one of his scolding notes in my fortune cookie, Allison, Allison?"

"You know I don't tattle."

"That's why you're so much fun to tease."

It wasn't her teasing that bothered me most right then. It was the scornful way she talked about Grandfather. "You and Aunt Bee don't like him the way he is, so why come over here all the time lately?" In the middle of my question my brain heard somebody come out of the library and shut the door. But my mouth went right on and finished the sentence.

Aunt Bee was beside me before I stopped. I guess she could tell we were having an argument. She said, "Now what, Allison?" as though if one person was at fault it had to be me.

I didn't say anything but Carolina did. "When I'm having fun she always comes banging in and wrecks everything." She put on a good act, looking honest and hurt at the same time.

"When I left you and Melody out here I told you to be quiet. What did she bang in on?"

74

"We were just playing. You know, Mother."

"No, I do not know, Carolina, that is why I ask." Listening to Aunt Bee and Carolina talking at each other made me glad all over again Mama is my mother.

"Me and Melody—"

"Melody and I, Carolina."

"Melody and I were just pretending."

"You're being evasive again, Carolina. I won't have it. What were you pretending?"

Carolina took a long breath as if she could put off answering. Then she said, "We were invited to a dance. We came downstairs to meet our dates like we were in high heels and long dresses. If we haven't practiced, we won't know how to do it when it's time." She moved her hands as if there was more she didn't have words for. But the words she had said scared me. I could picture an older Carolina coming down those stairs. I was afraid I understood that clue.

"I will not hear any nonsense about dates. I shall not allow you to go with boys for a long time and I do not want you thinking I will. Where is Melody now?"

"She went outside. It wasn't fun once Allison came."

"You find her and wait for me by the car." Carolina walked down the stairs with her chin up. I could tell she still had on her imaginary dancing dress and high heels. When she got where Aunt Bee couldn't see, she made an ugly face.

My aunt said, "Allison, you simply have not measured up to Godolphin standards lately. What, for instance, must people think of your disgraceful eye? Though I hesitate to step in uninvited, someone must assume the burden of keeping you in line. Now, on top of everything else, I find you bothering Grandfather, arguing in his hall."

"I wouldn't ever bother Grandfather," I said. "Never."

"Don't answer me back, Allison."

"But you aren't being fair."

The Bulldozer ignored that. Like Daddy said, she doesn't let logic get in her way.

"There is an old maxim that suits this occasion. I advise you to adopt it and put it to use: Anger Is Quelled By Counting. Now, I want you to count to one hundred."

I looked at my feet. Did I have to do this? It was so childish. But she kept standing there, waiting, so I knew I did. I started counting to myself as fast as I could. Instead of quelling anger, each number was making me madder.

"Allison! I asked you to count."

"I am counting." I had a hard time not yelling at her. "I'm already at fifty-one."

"Out loud. I want to hear you." She tapped her white patent leather shoe on each word.

"Fifty-one, fifty-two, fifty-three—"

"No, Allison. How provoking you are! From the beginning."

It's a long way from one to one hundred when someone is glaring at you like an angry policeman. The only noise in the hall was my numbers bounding off the ceiling, mixing with the clicks of the hall clock. I got so interested in the sound pattern I lost my place. "You missed seventy-seven," Aunt Bee said. "Shall I have to wait here while you start over again?"

"No. Seventy-seven, seventy-eight, seventy-nine—"

When I got to one hundred she said, "Now, I suggest you go home and get a good night's sleep. Maybe you will wake up tomorrow in a better mood." She shooed me out the door. But no matter what she said, I wasn't going home. I needed to talk to Robby. I knew now what she and Carolina were up to.

Melody and Carolina were leaning on Aunt Bee's car. As I passed they clapped their hands and stamped their feet and swung around together in perfect time chanting:

> "Ally, Ally, Allison,
> Always spoiling someone's fun
> Makes you hold your nose and run,
> Allison, Allison, Allison—UGH!"

Though it was hard to do, I made myself walk slowly as I went by them. I whistled and acted as if they weren't there, but their laughter hurt. They started chanting again as Aunt Bee started the motor. I was so mad she didn't make them stop that I didn't even pretend I was going home. I headed straight for Robby's. He was in the alley behind his house playing handball against the garage door with Pip and John.

"Great. Here comes Allison," John said. "Now we can play teams."

We played until it grew too dark to see the ball. I didn't get a chance to talk to Robby alone. He was spending the night with Pip and the three of them jogged away together.

Walking home I wondered what Carolina and Melody would think if they knew how I spent the evening. Let them pretend going dancing with boys. I was the one who had Pip and John for friends.

# 10

## *Robby and I Decide to Blab*

I rode around on my bike the next morning looking for Robby. Finally I found him in the alley between R and S streets heading home from Pip's. He wasn't getting far. He was trying to walk and keep a tennis ball in the air with his feet. Whenever the ball hit the ground, he'd go back to where he'd been. "I've gone all over town looking for you," I told him. "I've figured out what Aunt Bee's plot is."

"You have?" He forgot the ball. It landed in the border of Mrs. Graves' vegetable garden among the tomato plants.

"I'm sure I have. You know how Carolina's been prying

79

into everything at Grandfather's house? That's clue one. And last night she had Melody over there. They were parading down the hall stairs as if they were meeting dates to go dancing. There aren't any stairs at her house, so why would she need to practice coming down them? That's clue number two. And night before last The Bulldozer was pacing off Grandfather's dining room the way people do when they're thinking of buying a new rug. That's clue three. She jumped a mile when she saw me watching."

"They have their nerve. They treat Grandfather's house like it belongs to them." He sounded disgusted.

"That's what I'm talking about. I bet they're planning to move in with him."

"Them? There? They couldn't!"

"They only have to ask him. He'll agree if he thinks it's best for them. And when they get settled they'll start to dust everything up, including him and his books. Before long he'll feel he's in their way. I was wrong, Robby, when I said you can't walk in on a father and blab about his daughter. We've got to do it."

Robby thought so, too. He felt around for his ball among the tomatoes. He couldn't find it right away, and Mrs. Graves came and watched him through her back screen. She waved him closer so she wouldn't have to shout. "If you want tomatoes, Robby, please ask me first." She said it real low. She's always having to whisper at people between one and three o'clock. Her baby wakes up from his nap if anybody raises their voice on R Street.

"I was getting my ball, Mrs. Graves." He held it up so she could see.

She opened her door wider. "I'm glad it wasn't you two stealing my tomatoes. Someone has been. Come in. Have something to eat." We ate lemon bars and drank limeade on her side porch, whispering, glad to put off going to face Grandfather.

"Where are you two headed next?" Mrs. Graves asked. We got the hint it was time to go. We stood up, brushing off the powdered sugar that had drifted all over.

"To Grandfather's. We have to tell him something," Robby said. I poked him, afraid he'd say too much.

"If you'll wait a minute I'll cut a bouquet for him." We followed her into the flower garden beside the house. She snipped giant marigolds and snap dragons and floppy cosmos and hollyhocks and gathered them into a clump. Their smells mixed together into spice. She whispered about how she'd known Grandfather since she was our size. Wrapping the flowers in a plastic bag from the Cleanerama, she patted my shoulder. "You're looking more like your mother every day, Allison." I'll swear my nose twitched in alarm when she said it.

We left, me pushing my bike and worrying about my nose, Robby kicking his ball up at every step. It was like walking along with a puppet that was having all its strings jerked. I'd say, "We've got to warn him." Robby would answer, between kicks, "He's—got—to—know."

But when we were with Grandfather in his kitchen, it

wasn't easy to start. I handed him the flowers. "Find a vase for them, please," he said. "Have you had your lunch?" He was heating tomato soup. When we shook our heads he let us choose the kind we wanted from the can cupboard. Robby took chicken with rice. I picked alphabet. That meant dirtying three separate pans, but Grandfather's that way. He doesn't mind a mess if you get what you want.

His kitchen hasn't changed since Katy Rose died except that Grandfather put in the ceiling fan that was turning above us. It wasn't cooling the air much but it gave off a cosy whirr. Robby took crackers from the old stand-up cupboard that leans out so far from the kitchen wall you're uneasy walking past it. I'm glad Grandfather hasn't bought a new one. It shows how this bare kitchen looked when Katy Rose was filling it with good food and the clatter of dishes. Would it be better for Grandfather to have Aunt Bee living here, cooking for him? I thought about that for a while but decided it wouldn't. She's always trying new diets and he's already as thin as a nail file.

Grandfather poured the soup into three mugs and said, "You look as if you've been whipped. What's happened?" Still we couldn't bring ourselves to accuse The Bulldozer right out. He sipped his soup. Steam rose up off his mug and covered his glasses. Having his eyes hidden made me able to start.

"We're afraid," I said.

"Of what?"

"Aunt Bee and Carolina," Robby said.

"You're talking foolishness." He took off his glasses and wiped them with his handkerchief. I couldn't look at him with his eyes uncovered.

"We aren't fooling," I said into my alphabet soup, "but it may sound that way to you."

"Why don't you forget you started this conversation? We could finish our lunch and play three-handed Rummy in the garden."

"No, Grandfather, because it's really important." I took a deep breath and Robby gave me a thumbs-up sign. "Aunt Bee says you've begun acting really old, though nobody else thinks you have. And she says someone needs to manage you because of the Godolphin image. And we're afraid she'll try to make you different. And we want you just the way you are."

"And we think," Robby added, pushing ahead a lot faster than I'd meant to, "she's planning to ask you to let her and Carolina live here with you. If they do they'll spoil everything." There. It was said.

"Name seven things they'll spoil." Grandfather's always saying, "Name seven things," to make us think. It's kind of a game.

"One," I said, "they'll pick up your books. They don't understand it's comfortable seeing them lie around."

"Two," Robby said, "we won't be welcome here anymore."

"I doubt Two," said Grandfather. "You know I'll always welcome you."

"Three," I went on, feeling hopeless. He didn't understand what a difference The Bulldozer would make. "Aunt Bee keeps everything so clean at her house it makes you feel you're messing up just looking at it. She'll do that here."

"Four. Me and Al wouldn't feel it was our place. Aunt Bee wouldn't feel it was either." That was the same thing he'd said in Two. He was wasting our reasons.

"Five. They want to change things. We want them to stay the way they are."

Grandfather held up his hand to stop us. "That's enough. You aren't trying to see it from their point of view. They need a larger place. And things do change, Allison. You can't stop that."

"You can't let them," I cried. "What Aunt Bee said isn't true. You aren't either headed for your second childhood." I put my hand over my mouth, but it was too late. For the first time I understood why adults are always warning kids not to eavesdrop.

"I'm sure Bee didn't say that, Allison. People don't say that kind of thing in front of children. You've misunderstood." He was like Mama and Daddy in August. He wasn't hearing.

"Anyway, they don't love you the way we do," Robby said.

"They have their own way. Everyone's way is different."

Grandfather finished his soup. He set his mug on the sink with a bang, and I got up and washed it out. I could see we were making him mad.

Through the rush of water I heard Robby say, "They certainly have a nutty way. It's wrong to go talking about the people in your family behind their backs the way Aunt Bee does. Or decide things without asking them first."

"Bee isn't the only one who's doing that."

"Oh, no. Poor Grandfather. Who else?" I asked.

"Whoever took my ties and shirts and slippers."

I felt a blush start. It crept up my neck and heated my face. But Robby wasn't embarrassed. "Me and Al did that. Aunt Bee had it in for you. So we decided to fix all the things about you she didn't like. That way she wouldn't have anything left to complain about."

Grandfather leaned his elbows on the table and stared at us. It wasn't a very kind look. "Did you think, as you're accusing your Aunt Bee of thinking, that I was too old to take care of myself?" Until I heard him say it, I hadn't realized that was exactly how we'd acted. I let Robby explain. I felt too bad to say anything.

"We tried to take care of things so she'd let you alone."

"Your thinking was muddled, Robby. You didn't want her to change me so you thought you'd change me, instead. How could I stand up for myself not knowing what was going on?"

"You didn't have to. We were standing up for you."

Robby still didn't see we'd done anything to be ashamed of. How did it feel, I wondered, to suddenly find your family treating you as if you were too old to take care of yourself? My only hint was the way Carolina had treated me lately, teasing and getting her friends to so I felt all the girls were against me. I hadn't cried in a long time. But I cried for Grandfather then.

"You two back off and let me handle this myself," Grandfather said. He was acting like a different person. Lots of times he's far away in his own thoughts. But he looked so steely we knew he was absolutely in charge. "Promise?"

We promised. But as we left, even though it might make him madder, I had to say how I felt. "I still hope you don't let them move in here. It would be like living with two icicles."

Mama was making strudel when I got home. The kitchen smelled of apples and nutmeg. "Can we talk?" I asked, pinching off a piece of the dough. Even though it was August, she might hear me since she was alone.

"I can always talk, that's the thing I'm best at." She smiled. "Wash your hands before you sneak any more bites."

"I meant me talk and you listen."

Mama dampened a cloth and laid it over her pastry. She pulled up a stool and sat down. "I'm listening."

"Nothing is turning out right."

"Like what?"

"Grandfather's gotten mad at me twice lately. Even when I was trying to help him, he told me to mind my own business. That isn't the way he usually is. I'm scared for him."

Mama pulled me over beside her, and I stood in the circle of her arm looking at her bright hair. There was flour in it where she'd brushed it back. "What are you afraid of?"

"I think Aunt Bee plans to ask Grandfather to let her and Carolina move in with him. He'll probably say yes because he always does what the family wants. And she cares so much what people think about all of us, she won't let him go on being himself. She'll put away his books and make him slick himself up. And nothing will ever be the same, ever again."

Mama squeezed me. "She's already asked him. She asked him last night. She came by to tell me about it."

"What did you say to her, Mama?"

"I just listened."

"Did she tell what he answered? If he said yes it's the end of everything."

"He told her he'd think about it and let her know after the fortune cookies." She put her finger under my chin and turned it so my eyes were looking right into hers. "It would be a big change for you and Robby."

"It would be awful. I hate changes and this would change everything. Can't we do anything to stop her, Mama?"

87

She shook her head. "We have to stand back and trust Grandfather to make the right decision." That was just what Grandfather'd said. I wondered if Mama was as worried as I was about the way he'd decide.

She pulled the cloth off her dough and began stretching it again. As I turned to go upstairs she stopped me with the goodbye she and Daddy always use. "Did I ever tell you I love you?"

Of course she has, a thousand times, but I gave their answer, "No, never."

And she said, like she says to Daddy, "Well, I'm telling you now."

I climbed the stairs, kicking at them, worrying. I touched Katy Rose's clock and it chimed twice. "It's something about time you're supposed to teach me, isn't it? Is it that time changes everything?" But the clock wasn't giving any hints.

I went back to the stairs and called down, "Why does everybody smile when they talk about Katy Rose? People say she was so sweet. But what does that mean?"

Mama came and stood at the bottom of the stairs, holding her hands curled up in front of her so she wouldn't get flour on things. "People were comfortable with Grandmother. Everyone knew she liked them just the way they were."

"Then it wasn't only because she was beautiful?"

"No. Beauty alone doesn't get you far. What mattered was, she was so kind."

"Do you suppose that's the lesson Grandfather wants Carolina to learn?"

"It may be. Have you figured out yours yet?"

"No, but I keep wondering about it. Do you know what it is?"

Mama didn't answer. She'd already gone back to her strudel. I wondered if she realized, when she told how kind Katy Rose was, that she was giving a good description of herself. On the inside she and Katy Rose were alike. On the outside Aunt Bee and Katy Rose were alike. As Robby had said, "Insides are what count."

## II

# *What the Preacher's Warning Meant*

I dragged around after that. Working on Grandfather had helped me forget my own worries. But they were there waiting for me, and when I didn't have him to work on anymore, they blew up like giant balloons. "Name seven," Grandfather would have said. I couldn't name seven but I could name five. One, the threat of my nose. Two, Carolina's teasing. Three, not feeling ready for Junior High. Four, the lesson Grandfather wanted me to learn. Five, my black eye. I didn't have a solution for even one of them.

The fortune cookie dinner was only one week away. And

two days after that, school would begin. Where could I find answers in time? Grandfather had said the Shakespeare quote had wisdom for a twelve-year-old. But I didn't want to think about that. Shakespeare had gotten me into enough trouble already.

The last days of August were slow and dull. Robby and I had used up all the summer fun in June and July. Tennis was left, but it was too hot for tennis. We'd saved swimming to carry us through the last month of vacation. Now the filter at the town pool was broken. Every kid in Godolphin-ville was feeling dried out because the repairs were taking forever.

I read the Oz books through again. And even wrote my pen pal, something I only do when I've run out of everything else. So I was glad when Robby called up and said to meet him after dinner at the factory field. The last baseball game of the season was going to be played, and he wanted to be in on the excitement.

When I got there a line of cars and pickups was bumping into the parking lot stirring up dust. A bigger crowd than usual poured into the stands. Even Reverend Kean was there and Lisa Pierce with Whiskey on his leash. Everybody'd come to see whether the Luxor Spear Carriers or the Godol-phinville Hot Shots would win the trophy. I found Robby at the concession stand. We bought snow cones and watched the bleachers fill up. Then we got a paper bucket of popcorn because the hot butter smelled so good.

The teams were ready to start when there was an interruption. Reverend Kean walked onto the field holding up his hands. His black suit made him stand out among the players in their uniforms. Stopping between the second baseman and the pitcher the preacher began to boom, "Dear people, dear people, quiet, quiet, quiet." He hushed that crowd like it was Mrs. Graves' baby. His words rolled across the field, even shutting up the kids playing behind the stands. "Please join me in a prayer for rain," he thundered. "You farmers must have it to save your crops. We townspeople know your need and want to help."

A man cheered in the Luxor section. Another stood and shouted, "Get on with the ball game." There were hisses and boos and some loud clapping. Was Reverend Kean planning to give us the wind and clouds and rain and hail and thermals and sunlight and shadow and maybe even continental drift again? If he did, he'd start a riot. But he didn't seem to worry what people thought of him. He was like Mama and Grandfather who go on being themselves no matter what people say.

The preacher bowed his head. Almost everybody else did, too. He prayed in his bass drum voice for rain and for the farmers. Then he gave God thanks for His goodness. It was over in one minute. The little kids beside me who were watching for his prayer to bring up thunderclouds in the west said he should have worked at it longer.

Fans pounded their hands and shouted, "Come on, rain."

Except the ones yelling, "Batter up." Reverend Kean trotted off the field. Until the drought was over it looked like he'd be praying up his storm wherever there were people to pray with.

Mr. Pierce was our first batter. He swung and hit into left field. Whiskey broke away from Lisa and chased after his master trailing his leash. Mr. Pierce stopped on first base and yelled, "Lisa McCalley Pierce, get Whiskey off this field! I'll send him to the dog pound if he gets loose again." Bright red, Lisa ran in circles trying to catch hold of the leash. Mrs. Pierce helped, standing up in the front row calling, "Here, Whiskers. Here, Whiskers." The fans loved it. They hammered their feet and yelled, "Yeah, dog," until the air rattled.

Robby had his bat and ball. When the Hot Shot-Spear Carrier game got boring, we rounded up some guys and started a game of our own in back of the stands. Later Melody and Carolina came strolling by with their hands behind them. Lisa Pierce was with them, and Whiskey, pulling to get to the old napkins and cans under the bleachers. A boy shouted, "Hang onto that dog, Lisa McCalley Pierce, or I'll send you to the dog pound." Lisa turned red for the second time that night, but pretended she didn't hear. Like me she wasn't going to admit the teasing hurt.

Carolina and Melody laid what they were carrying down in the grass. They leaned against the posts of the grandstand to watch us play. Someone they liked came to bat and they cheered. When I was up they chanted:

> "Tomboy Allison, what a guy
> Look at her
> Disgusting eye,
> Allison, Allison, Allison—UGH!"

But I made a two-base hit anyhow. And some of the kids told them to cut it out or go away.

The game went on. It was growing dark. Only Pip and me were left to bat. Heat lightning started up down south and the lights on the field flashed on. Then Carolina walked over. "May I pitch?" she asked. It wasn't as crazy an idea as you might think because Carolina is as good an athlete as I am. She just doesn't like games as much as I do. She looked cool and clean all in white. And fancy because she had on some of Melody's junk jewelry. The guys kind of stared around at each other and shrugged. And John said, "Why not?"

She stepped to the mound and caught the ball the first baseman threw her. She zinged it over the plate, and though it was now almost dark because the field lights weren't any help where we were, Pip hit it for a three-base run.

"We better stop," Robby shouted. "It's too hard to see."

"Just one more," Carolina said. "I'll hurry."

I stepped up to the plate. Carolina stood out in her white shorts and blouse but everything else was dim. "Ready?" she asked me.

"Go ahead."

She pitched. I swung and connected. Splat. In the dark I couldn't see what I'd hit but it was all over me, in my hair, in my face. And shrieks of laughter were rising from the girls. They ran together and lined up and began their cheer-leading motions:

> "Allison looks like a sack of potatoes
> She looks even worse
> When she's smeared with tomatoes,
> Allison, Allison, Allison—UGH!"

A man leaned over the top row of seats and called, "You kids shut up down there. You're making too much noise." The girls turned and ran, dragging Whiskey. John and Pip grabbed up the tomatoes left behind in the grass and threw them. There was another splat, like mine, and Melody screamed.

Some of the guys were rolling around on the ground laughing, but Pip came up and grabbed the sleeve of my shirt. "Listen Allison. You've got to do something. Either let me hit 'em or you do it. If they're still keeping this up when we go over to Luxor you'll have that whole big school on your back."

"I know. I know. I just haven't decided yet what to do." Tears of desperation made it hard for me to see Pip.

"You only have till next Monday. John and I'll be glad to settle this for you. How about it?"

"I'll let you know."

"Well, you better hurry up." He sounded really mad. As much at me as he was at Carolina and the others.

The slimy juice of the tomato was beginning to dry, leaving seeds stuck all over me. I knew now what Reverend Kean meant when he told me to watch out for tomatoes. And who had been practicing throwing them against the wall of the library. And who had been stealing them from Mrs. Graves' garden. Making his calls at night in his dark clothes he must have seen Carolina and Melody and Lisa without them knowing.

Robby pushed between Pip and me and said, "Come on, let's get Coke floats at The Big Dipper." We ran off together like always, me and the guys.

On the way home afterwards, Robby and I passed the rental house that's kitty-corner from where I live. The yard light was on and bugs fought each other for a place close to the bulb. On the back sidewalk three girls were jumping rope. I suppose they were the renter's daughters come to visit. I hadn't seen any of them before. Yet as they jumped they chanted:

> "Allison, Allison, yes indeed,
> Pigeon-toed and
> Knocky-kneed,
> Allison, Allison, Allison—UGH!"

One girl jumped out and a smaller one jumped in.

"Crybaby Allison suck your thumb
No one likes you
You're so dumb,
Allison, Allison, Allison—UGH!"

They looked at us as we passed their yard, Robby bouncing his bat against the tree trunks. We waved like you do in Godolphinville whether you know people or not. They waved back. I'm sure they didn't know I was the one they were chanting about. But they made me feel like I'd been crowned Miss Unpopular at the state fair. Even people who'd never seen me were picking up Carolina's verses and learning to dislike Allison Cox.

"Everything's a mess, Robby."

"You're right. Everything is."

As we separated at the corner Reverend Kean came along. "How are the tomato wars?" he asked me.

"Terrible."

"Come on, I'll walk you home." We went across the street and stood at the end of my sidewalk talking. Suddenly I found myself telling him everything that happened with Carolina, even though part of my mind was saying, "Hey, you promised you wouldn't tattle." But the other part was answering back, "It's okay. Ministers never tell secrets if you ask them not to." So I asked him not to.

For once, he didn't tangle me up in words. He listened. I finished and waited for him to tell me what I had to do.

But he only said, "You'll work it out," and started describing what Junior High would be like. Then he walked off. I went in the house wishing I had as much confidence in me as he did.

# 12

## Reunion Day Clashes

Katy Rose's clock woke me, striking eight times. It was the morning of the town reunion. This was the day I was supposed to know the lesson the clock had to teach me. "What is it? What is it?" I asked myself as I pulled on the ruffled dress and went downstairs.

Mama believes in bringing up kids on love and compliments. But she couldn't think of anything complimentary to say when I walked in the dining room. My ruffles drooped and so did I. I'd hoped Reverend Kean's prayers for rain would finally be answered so I could hide the dress under my raincoat. But the sun was as bright as a poppy.

Besides the way the dress looked, there was my eye. At first it had just been red and blue and swollen. But each day since Robby hit me the colors had grown brighter. By Reunion Day it was at its best, or worst. There was purple over the cheek bone and yellow around the edges, and the place the ring hit looked almost green. People I met couldn't help but ask how it happened. Unfortunately, Mama doesn't just believe in bringing up kids on love and compliments. She believes in bringing them up honest, too.

"What will I tell people?" I asked her. "I don't want to say Robby hit me. And everybody is going to ask."

"Make a joke about it," Mama said. "But I don't want you lying."

"What joke, for instance?"

"Something will occur to you. Everyone has inner resources that spring into action in an emergency." She was listening to me but not really hearing. If she'd been hearing, she'd have known I was desperate.

"You stick with me, Kid, I'll protect you," Daddy said. But I knew he'd be over with the Lions Club talking about fishing. Or else he'd be with the factory people talking about paint and ash wood. Or he'd walk around holding hands with Mama, laughing with old friends. None of that included me.

Mama delivered her two apple strudels to the school gym where lunch was to be served. Then we drove to the factory for the ceremony. On Reunion Day they remember the history of Godolphin's Fine Furniture Company. Without the factory to give people work, our town and the ones around it might have withered away.

When we went in, I saw Grandfather and Uncle Robert and the president of the workers union on the balcony that hangs above the work space. Below them the machines sat silent and a crowd stood among them. People who'd been born in Godolphinville or worked at the factory were all around us with their families. Some had come from far away. They held signs telling where they lived now. I saw "I Come from California" on one sign and "Athens, Georgia" on another.

"Did you notice how nice Grandfather looks in his new tie we bought him?" It was Robby pushing through the crowd to stand beside us.

Before I could answer Uncle Robert stepped to the edge of the balcony and began speaking. He took a long time. He would probably have taken longer if the factory had chairs so we could sit down. People kept shifting around to rest their tired legs. One shift split the crowd and I saw Carolina halfway down the long building. I knew then why Aunt Bee had chosen the pink dress. On Carolina it looked old-fashioned. In it she'd remind people of Aunt Bee when she was Carolina's age. Older ones might think of Katy Rose when she was young. The frilly dress and the way Carolina had her black hair pinned back with a silver pin was like a picture from Grandfather's photo album.

But Carolina had grown too much this year for the dress to look right. She was too old, now, for all those ribbons and bows. For the first time she wasn't the model of how the prettiest girl at the reunion ought to look.

When the speeches ended the crowd moved toward the school gym. Before we could get separated Mama said, "Remember to spend time with the great-aunts. They'll want to see how you've grown."

Daddy put his hand on my shoulder. "Don't go worrying how you look. Mama and I think you're fine the way you are, black eye, pink dress and all."

"I know you do, Daddy, but that doesn't count." We left them and Robby worked through the crowd dragging me. I thought he wanted to get lunch before all the drumsticks were gone. But when we reached a corner, he pushed me into it out of the crowd. I realized he was angry.

"So what does count with you, Allison Cox?" he said as if I was somebody he didn't know very well and didn't like at all.

"What are you talking about?"

"That's the second time you've said that lately, Al. I've had it with you."

I still didn't know what he was talking about. "Said what?"

"Said, 'But that doesn't count.' You just said it to your dad as if hearing he's for you one hundred percent means nothing at all. I wish my dad would say that to me. And you said it after the birthday party, too, remember? When I said I'd like you no matter what your nose did."

"I didn't mean what you and Daddy told me wasn't important."

"Then why say it?" I was trying to think up a way to explain. But Robby didn't wait to hear it. "You're getting more like The Bulldozer every day. You spend time worrying what other people think and don't care what people close to you think."

I opened my mouth to answer but he stomped off. Maybe it was a good thing. The last time I argued with him when he said I was like Aunt Bee, he'd given me my black eye. Was I getting like her?

Reunion Day is an even noisier Godolphinville celebration than the Fourth of July. People keep shouting to friends they haven't seen for a long time. Two women will give matching screams and push through the crowd to hug each other. Drivers honk at people walking. Walkers shout back. Everybody eats too much and talks too loud and laughs enough to last till next year.

Lunch was spread out on tables covered with white paper. Twisted ropes of vines and flowers looped across their fronts. I took a place in line and a paper plate, wishing Robby hadn't stalked off and left me.

Behind me two ladies from my church were talking about Reverend Kean. Did Daddy's warning about not listening without telling you were there count in a crowded gym? Just to be safe I turned around and coughed. The ladies both said, "Hello, Allison," and went right on with their conversation so I guessed it was okay to listen.

Mrs. Formey said, "You'd think that brash young preacher would be embarrassed praying everywhere. He'll be standing up in The Purple Plaza next, asking us to pray for rain between the coming attractions and the feature film."

Mrs. Meinhoff didn't agree. "I admire his enthusiasm. Our minister could use a little of it. At least that Reverend Kean would keep my husband from falling asleep during the sermon." Everybody seemed to have an opinion about everybody else and the opinions didn't match up. Maybe a person just had to make up their own mind and stop worrying what other people thought.

Mama's strudel was gone by the time I reached the dessert table. So I just added cherry pie with ice cream to my potato salad and drumsticks and Jell-O and applesauce and went outside. In spite of home-grown tomatoes, geraniums, and barbeque sauce perfuming the air, the smell of gym lockers was getting to me in that hot building.

People were eating and greeting in the schoolyard and in the park past the school. I stood against the wall of the gym and ate and watched the crowd.

Right after lunch the games began. I wasn't in the mood for races and contests after my argument with Robby. But he found me and started in talking just as if he hadn't been yelling at me an hour before. "Will you do the three-legged race with me? There's a great kite for the prize. It's silver foil and has colored streamers for a tail."

We met The Bulldozer when we were walking through the park to sign up. Carolina tagged behind her pouting. "Here you are, Allison," Aunt Bee said. "I want you and Carolina to run the three-legged race together. It will make a lovely snapshot, you girls in your pink dresses breaking the tape." I could tell Carolina hated the idea.

"I'm sorry, Aunt Bee, I'm doing the three-legged with Robby. But how about taking a picture of Carolina and me right here?" That suggestion made Carolina look happier.

"Carolina has no partner for the race, Allison. I want a shot of it for her scrapbook." I knew that scrapbook. Aunt Bee has pictures in it of all the things Carolina has won. She must be expecting Carolina to win again.

"I promised Robby. I know you wouldn't want me to break my promise."

That stopped The Bulldozer, but only for a minute. "I am sure Robert Junior will be kind enough to let you do this for Carolina." She looked him in the eye and tapped her foot. That day she had on red high-heeled shoes with the toes cut out. They didn't make any noise on the grass. Still, it made me just as nervous as when she tapped her white patent leathers at me on the bare floor of Grandfather's front hall.

It must have made Robby nervous, too. He said, "Oh, okay. But I wanted to win the kite."

"The girls will win the kite for you."

"I'm not sure we can. Robby and I have had practice running together. But Carolina and I haven't."

Carolina snapped, "I'm the best runner in our class. Faster than you any day." Actually we always tie for first.

Robby tapped his foot as if he was picking up bad habits from Aunt Bee. "Me and Al won last year, Carolina. You didn't come anywhere close."

"That was because of Lisa. She's slow."

Aunt Bee acted like we were all happy with her arrangements. She pulled a big scarf out of her purse and tied Carolina's knee to mine. She pulled out another and tied our ankles together. One scarf was lavender, the other soft green. Neither one clashed with pink. I could see she'd planned this picture-taking before she left home. "You girls get some practice while the sack races are being run. And Allison, when you see me ready to snap the picture, turn toward Carolina so your black eye will not show."

"How can we win if I'm not looking where I'm going?" I asked.

Carolina asked a lot of things. "Why do I have to do the race with her? Don't you know I'm too old for this? How can I run when it's so hot?" She even said she hated the babyish pink dress. But when The Bulldozer doesn't want to answer, you might as well be talking to a piece of Godolphin's Fine Furniture. She hurried away toward the finish line. Robby ran after her. I guess he wanted to keep an eye on his kite.

"We're going to win this race, you hear?" Carolina said between her clenched teeth.

"I'm only running with you to get the kite for Robby. Promise he'll get the kite?" No matter what Aunt Bee said, I wasn't going to run the race unless Carolina promised.

"He can have the stupid kite. I don't care. Stop arguing. We need to warm up."

When the race was called we were first at the starting line. When the gun went off we stepped out as if we'd run a hundred three-legged races together. Winning looked like a sure thing until a team of boys came up behind and bumped us, passing. They turned and grinned, thinking they'd won. But you don't grin at Carolina if you want to beat her. She took a spurt and I spurted with her. By a quarter inch we were first across the finish line.

The Bulldozer got her snapshot, but she got a straight-on view of my black eye. I wasn't going to be a complete marshmallow and let her have everything her way. Still tied together, Carolina and I ran up to the judges' table to claim Robby's prize.

Mr. Graves handed the kite carefully across to me. "That's a real beauty. I bought it last week when I was in San Francisco. I'm glad you won it, Allison."

"We won it for Robby, Mr. Graves. He's going to love it. Come on, Carolina. I want to take it to him before something happens to it." Holding the kite in both hands I turned to look for Robby. As I took a step, Carolina jerked her leg back, and mine, tied to it, went along. The jolt threw me forward, off balance. I fell on the kite pulling Carolina to her knees.

"Allison, Allison," Carolina said, "too bad you didn't look where you were going. Now you've ruined Robby's kite." Before I could get up she slipped off the scarves and was gone in the crowd.

Robby came and stood staring down at the smashed kite. His face was long and sad. "I saw that, Al. That skunk planned to do it all the time. She always wins." He picked up the tangle of streamers and silver. The kite would never fly. It was too badly torn even to hang up as a decoration.

"I give you my word, Robby, somehow I'm going to pay her back."

# 13

## Come On,
## You Inner Resources

"What happened to your eye, Allison?" My sixth-grade teacher stood before me. I was speechless. Here was Robby right beside me, the broken kite in his hands. He was going to have this teacher when school started. I couldn't say he'd hit me.

I cleared my throat while my mind rummaged around hunting for an answer. Then just the way Mama said they would, my inner resources made an idea pop in my mind. "Running head on into something can do lots of damage, can't it, Mrs. Staba? Would you like to see my eye up close?"

I heard the silver kite rattle as Robby and I waited for her answer. She said, "Not right now," turned, and left. All afternoon I used that same reply to questions about my eye. It worked on everybody until the great-aunts cornered me.

Robby had gone to show the broken kite to Pip and I was playing Hangman with John on the side of the gym. I didn't notice the aunts wandering through the crowd with coffee cups in their hands.

Grandfather's sisters are older than he is. They're so old that the only time they come to Godolphinville anymore is for the reunion. Each year Great-aunt Tilla seems more near-sighted and Great-aunt Myrtle deafer and Great-aunt Fanny May even stranger than she was the year before. It's hard to think of things to say to them. Great-aunt Myrtle keeps chirping, "Speak up. Don't swallow your words." Then people turn and glare at me because they think I'm not showing respect for my elders. And all the time I'm yelling as loud as I can.

Great-aunt Myrtle turned to the others and shrilled, "See that dress? This must be John Robert's other granddaughter." People nearby looked to see what she meant by that.

I touched each of their hands in turn. "I'm Allison," I hollered. Over my head they talked family history, worked out that I was Bee's, no, Fran's daughter, and decided I was eight years old. They acted like I was the one who was deaf and strange.

Fanny May put her mouth close to Aunt Myrtle's ear.

"Pinky, inky, blue and blacky eye," she piped in her thin, old voice.

Myrtle looked where Fanny pointed. "She's right. Just look at that eye."

Tilla put her nose close to mine. "You do have a black eye, poor little one. Tell us all about what happened."

I knew "Running head on into something can do lots of damage" wasn't going to work this time. The great-aunts wouldn't be happy till they had the whole story to take home and talk about all winter. Great-aunt Tilla's nearsighted eyes peered into mine searching for the truth. Mama's "I don't want you lying" echoed in my head.

My shoulders were slumped from embarrassment. I hated to give Robby away but there was no way out. At least he wasn't there to hear me but a lot of other people were. Poor Robby. I straightened up to deliver the true story and my head bumped the bottom of Myrtle's cup. Coffee poured down me like a river. It stained the dress, browned the ribbons, and wet through everything I had on. My socks mushed in my shoes.

The great-aunts forgot my eye. They set their cups on the ground and felt in their rusty black purses. Myrtle and Tilla pulled out embroidered handkerchiefs. They dabbed at me, murmuring sadly. Fanny May fumbled with a tiny bottle that had a gold stopper. She uncorked it and pushed it under my nose. "Breath deeply," she ordered. I did, and nearly strangled. It was ammonia. I was suffocating.

Choking, I darted from them ignoring their shouts and ran around the corner. I would have been smarter to stay and be petted among the old aunts. As I dived behind the gym, I saw that Carolina and Melody and Lisa Pierce were there before me practicing their cheers. Oh, squash!

"Here's your twin, Caro," said Melody. "Poor us."

"She looks just as bad as always," said Lisa, pointing her thumb toward my stained dress.

Was it the ammonia that did it or was it my inner resources? I'll never know. But whatever it was, I suddenly saw what I had to do to stop their teasing. I told Melody, "You and Lisa get out of here. I have to talk to Carolina alone."

Carolina said, "Talk? You and me? Forget it."

Melody said, "You're impossible, Allison. Who do you think you're bossing around?"

I grabbed hold of the long ropes of beads she was wearing. "I'm bossing you. And I mean it."

"Let go of my beads. They'll break and we'll have to pick them all up."

"I'll break more than that if you aren't out of here in two minutes." The three of them stared at me as if I'd lost my mind.

Carolina said, "You're the one who's getting out. Quit fooling around. We need to practice."

"I'm not fooling." I twisted the beads and one string popped, spraying fake red pearls all down Melody's front.

"Carolina, help!" Melody tried to pull away. A green

strand broke. "Look what she's doing. Hit her or something!"

"Anybody touches me and I'll yank these so hard every string will break." I tightened my hold on her beads and she stepped closer to keep them from pulling.

"Go on, Lisa," I said. "Get out." Lisa looked from Carolina to me to Melody. She started walking.

"Send somebody back to help," Melody called after her.

"Tell them to go away and stay away," I told Carolina.

She curled her lip. But Melody said, "Please, Caro. My dad brought some of these beads from Mexico. If they get broken, he'll be furious at me." A tear ran down her cheek.

"Oh, go on then, you chicken," Carolina said. "She wouldn't have broken them all. She'd be afraid to. She's as chicken as you are."

"If you go telling anybody, you'll be sorry." I let go of Melody, and she and Lisa sprinted out of there. They stopped by the corner of the gym as if to watch over Carolina's safety. But I made a run at them and they disappeared.

"So what's this all about Allison, Allison?" Carolina asked. I guess I'd made her curious acting so different from my usual self.

"It's about the chants. They stop today or else."

"Or else what? I suppose you're ready to tattle." She put on her high-hat look.

"I don't need to tattle. You're going to beg me to let you stop them before I'm through with you."

"Hah." I hadn't scared her at all. I looked at her awhile. "Quit staring," she said. I stared some more. "Well, go on. Say what you came for or I'm leaving."

I reached over and took hold of her dress at the neck. What had gotten into me? I was jerking everybody around. "You'll stay and listen until I'm good and ready to let you leave."

She slapped at me and tried to pull away but I had her anchored. "And if I don't?"

"I'll rip this front panel right out."

"Go ahead. Tear it up. I hate this dress."

"You'll also hate walking home through the crowd in your slip." She looked down and saw what I'd seen when I grabbed her neckline. If I jerked it hard enough, that whole lacy front might separate from the material on both sides. That persuaded her to settle down and listen. But I didn't talk for a few minutes. I just stared at her face. Then I said, "Turn your head to the side so I can look at your nose better."

"What for?"

"To see if it's started to grow." That was to pay her back for ruining Robby's kite.

"What are you talking about?"

"Didn't you know Mama got the Godolphin nose when she was in Junior High?"

"So?"

"So you and I may start growing it any minute."

114

"My mother didn't." But she cupped her hand over her nose. Her eyes were wide with horror.

"And now. About the chants," I said.

She must have been picturing what a difference the Godolphin nose would make if she did grow it. As far back as I could remember she'd been the prettiest girl in town. She certainly wouldn't be if she grew the nose. She stared off into space. Finally she said, "You thought that would make me stop the chants? From now on you're going to get them twice as hard for the way you bullied us this afternoon."

"No I'm not. They stop today or you and Lisa Pierce and Melody aren't going to be cheerleaders."

"What are you talking about? How could you stop us?"

"Easy. Reverend Kean told me about Junior High. You don't just have to be good at cheerleading to get on the squad. The class has to vote on the candidates. And the kids all vote for ones from their own elementary schools. Because at the beginning of the year, they don't know each other."

"And Godolphinville Elementary is the biggest school so we'll win."

"Not if the kids from Godolphinville don't vote for you, Caro, Caro."

"Why wouldn't they?"

"Because unless you promise me I'll never, ever hear another chant from you or anybody else, I'll tell them not to."

She laughed right out then. "And why would they listen to you? They think you're as dumb as I do."

"You're talking about girls. I'm talking about boys. You can't rule the Junior High like you've done over here unless they both vote for you. And the boys won't if I ask them not to. They're my friends. Not yours." At least Pip and John are, I added to myself, and maybe they'll help me persuade the others.

I could see that worried her. She frowned and chewed on the inside of her cheek. But being Carolina, she wasn't going to give in straight away. She had to argue awhile first. We must have looked pretty stupid standing there in our twin pink dresses, me holding hers by the neck ready to rip it up, she so angry her cheeks were like fire. And then, too, there was my black eye.

"So you're ready to trade the chants for the boys' votes?" she asked when she saw she wasn't going to talk me out of anything.

"Maybe."

"Maybe? That's what you wanted wasn't it Allison, Allison?"

"It's what you want. I haven't decided yet if it's what I want."

"Well, decide."

"Beg me." That was for pitching me the tomato.

Her head went up and she looked just like Aunt Bee for a minute, proud and sure about everything. But she must have wanted awfully much to be a cheerleader because after a couple of gulps and swallows she said in a small voice, "Please, Allison."

"Again."

"Please, Allison."

"I haven't decided yet." That was for all the mean verses she'd made up about me.

"When will you? It's important. I have to know what to tell Melody and Lisa." She was really begging that time.

"Tell them I'll let you know after the fortune cookies."

# 14

## *Looking for the Lesson*

For weeks I'd daydreamed about putting uppity Carolina in her place. If I manage to do that, I thought, I'll feel like I've won the state lottery. And for a while I did. But then the picture of Carolina standing there, begging me, began to run back and forth in my mind. It made me ashamed. I knew too well how she felt. I didn't want to treat her the way she'd treated me. I just wanted her and Lisa Pierce and Melody to let me alone.

I left the playground and wandered out through town. The schoolyard and park were still crowded with people.

Curbs were jammed with cars. Sheriff Joe Watson walked among them, on hand in case some kid got lost from his parents. But only two blocks away I walked past empty houses, along quiet streets. No children shouted on the slide behind the Methodist church. No one was washing cars under the elm trees or pulling weeds in their vegetable gardens. All Godolphinville was at the reunion, watching slide shows of other reunions, playing volleyball, filling up on root beer and talk.

The lonely streets were what I needed. I wanted time to myself to do some thinking. I wanted to figure out Grandfather's lesson before I read it in my fortune cookie.

I walked down the alley between R and Q streets and Whiskey Pierce greeted me with a bark. He stood with his paws on the top rail of his pen, his tail swinging. Leaning against his fence I patted his head and rubbed his neck. So many things had happened since the morning after my birthday party when Mrs. Pierce banged him with her broom. Among all those happenings there must be clues to what Grandfather wanted me to know.

Was his lesson about my nose? But unless Robby had told him, and Robby doesn't blab about me, Grandfather had absolutely no way of knowing I was worried about that. And standing there, running my hand down Whiskey's brown back, I realized something. I'd almost stopped thinking about my nose. My worry began to fade when Mama said of Katy Rose, "Beauty alone doesn't get you far. What counted was, she was so kind." So if by any chance that was his lesson, I'd already learned it from Mama.

It was more likely the lesson was about being afraid of Carolina's teasing. Grandfather had never seemed to know about that, either. But he has a mysterious way of finding out things we do to each other. We're surprised by that every year when we open our fortune cookies. Now the teasing was over, like the worry about my nose. Never again would I let Carolina build herself up by tearing me down.

Whiskey punched my arm with his sleek nose. I'd been so busy thinking, I forgot to pet him. I started in again, scratching behind his ears. He dropped down to rest his legs, and I sat on the grass to rest mine. Through the chain link fence around his kennel, we leaned against each other. He whined and I began to talk out loud so he'd know I was thinking about him.

"I've changed, Whiskey," I said. "I've changed a lot since the birthday party. Back then I wanted to stay eleven forever. I wanted to keep everything always the same like it was frozen in place. I don't feel that way anymore.

"Because if nothing had changed, I wouldn't have changed either. I wouldn't have found out I'm strong. I wouldn't know I have inner resources. I wouldn't have learned it's okay to be who I am no matter what people think.

"That must be why Grandfather gave me the clock with the quote. He wanted me to learn that change is coming, no matter how hard I fight it. It must be what I do with change that counts."

I reached through the fence and shook Whiskey's paw. "You know what, Dog? I'm ready for twelve. I'm ready for the Consolidated Junior High." Through the fence he licked my ear.

I left the Pierces' backyard and walked across the street to Grandfather's house. Whiskey's whine was the only sound on Front Street, that and my shoes scraping the pavement. The door stood open. I brushed off dog hairs before I went inside.

Grandfather was asleep in his tall library chair, a book lying face down on his stomach. There was a button off his collar and spots, like decorations, down his new tie. With his mouth open, his breath a gentle snore, his face all slumped in sleep, he looked older than old. I started to shake him awake so I wouldn't have to see those signs that time was changing him. But instead I stepped away. Whatever changes came, Grandfather would do a good job of handling them.

# 15

## *After the Fortune Cookies*

As I turned to leave, I bumped against the desk and Grandfather woke up. "Allison!" he said, smiling. His face looked like him again. He glanced at his watch. "It won't be time for dinner for another hour. Have you had enough reunion?"

"More than enough. It was the most educational reunion I've ever been to. I found out things today about myself I can hardly believe. And I think I've figured out the lesson you wanted me to learn."

"I thought you might, though it wasn't easy." He touched

my shoulder. "Why don't you go and help Miss Betty in the kitchen?"

Miss Betty Willson's fortune cookie dinner is the best meal we have all year. No wonder. Miss Betty is the best cook in Godolphinville. She used to work for Katy Rose and she still uses those old recipes to make foods we don't eat any other time. Chess pies, for instance, and corn relish. She cooks us a seven-course meal with special side dishes and even homemade chocolate mints after the last course.

Miss Betty was glad to have help. She let me shine serving spoons and chop salad. She showed me how to fold the heavy linen napkins so they looked like nesting birds. She also gave me tastes of everything. When it was nearly time to eat I put ice in the glasses. Grandfather came to watch us. Then he went and set place cards and his fortune cookies around the table.

At six o'clock we heard the family arriving. They rushed up the porch steps because the rain I had hoped for that morning was on the way. A wind had risen, blowing curtains of dust in front of it. Miss Betty had me serve hot cheese puffs to them in the living room.

"How come you get to help?" Carolina asked. I gave her the Want to trade? look, but she shook her head. "It's more fun to sit and watch you work." But her voice didn't have the snap and sneer I'd gotten used to that summer.

Miss Betty asked me to light the candles on the table. Then she announced dinner by ringing the gong in the hall.

There's something about hearing that gong that makes a person remember their manners. We filed into the dining room and quietly found our places.

Everyone else's fortune cookie looked just like always. But mine had a little envelope beside it as if Grandfather had so much advice to give me, he hadn't been able to squeeze it all inside. Was my character in that much need of shaping up? The thought made my appetite wilt.

There has to be lots of talk when we're working through one of Miss Betty's meals. Otherwise people eat too fast and fall out halfway through. So everybody chewed slowly and talked about the reunion during the French onion soup and shrimp cocktail and fresh pineapple salad. I found my appetite coming back, there was so much good food to use it on.

Aunt Bee asked why my dress was such a wreck. That started Mama and Daddy telling one funny story after another about the great-aunts. And I thought, even though they only pay half their attention to me in August, it's worth a lot.

Miss Betty passed tiny mounds of sherbet. "To clear your palates," she said. Then she served roast beef and duck in orange sauce. All the time my eyes kept swinging back and forth between the food on my plate and the envelope by my fortune cookie. At last Miss Betty came through the swinging door with a platter of cheeses and fruit. She set a slice of pie in front of each of us. When she went back to the kitchen, everyone looked toward Grandfather and he said, "It's fortune cookie time."

The cookies crackled as they were broken. Then there was only the sound of Carolina tearing her fortune into tiny scraps. She looked once at Grandfather, then seemed to slide down inside herself. And I knew she'd got a bad one.

I opened my envelope and read,

Allison,

At your birthday party you stood on the shore, unwilling to set sail into the future. You said, again and again, "I hate changes." But you set to work fighting the changes Aunt Bee proposed. And though I didn't agree with all you did, I was glad your fear hadn't made you helpless. You battled half your family and peppered the others with questions. You watched what people did and asked yourself, "Is that right?" All the time you were growing stronger and wiser. I'm proud of you. Your new self-confidence will carry you on to fortune.

Grandfather

P.S. Your Aunt Bee and Carolina aren't nearly as bad as you think. Copy your mama. Be kind to them.

It sounded just like Grandfather. I didn't show my fortune pleased me. I really am changing, I thought. I don't even want Carolina to know my fortune is better than hers.

Grandfather stood up. He always ends the fortune cookie dinner with a speech, all about the past year. But that night he was more interested in the future. "Tonight," he said, "is the beginning of many changes. Our girls are growing up and will be gone much of the time when school starts. I've decided it will be best for everyone if Bee and Carolina move over here to the family home. It's time the house had better care than I've been giving it. I hope you will be very happy here." Usually Aunt Bee is prim and formal but she actually grinned when Grandfather said that. But for me it was worse than being hit with another tomato. I hated what The Bulldozer and Carolina would do to Grandfather. Robby looked like Grandfather's words had turned him to ice. We'd neither of us believed he'd let them move in with him. Was this his good job of handling change? Tears were gathering behind my lids but I told my tear ducts to cut it out. I wasn't going to give Carolina the pleasure of seeing me cry.

Aunt Bee let out her breath as if she'd been holding it ever since she asked Grandfather about moving in. Mama clapped and then we all did. And Aunt Bee walked to the head of the table to hug Grandfather. She circled around so she could nudge Carolina. At first Carolina acted as if she was still too mad at Grandfather to care what he'd just announced. But then she blew him a kiss.

At that moment wind shook the house and the first rain-drops came tapping down. Then it was pouring. Daddy got up and closed the windows, trapping the heat inside. Some-where, I knew Reverend Kean was giving thanks.

Grandfather had more to say. "Earlier this month I gave Robby and Allison a verse to learn. Maybe they will say it with me." We repeated it as we had done after the birthday party before we kissed him good night at his door:

> " 'There is a tide in the affairs of men
> Which, taken at the flood, leads on to fortune;
> Omitted, all the voyage of their life
> Is bound in shallows and in miseries.' "

I still didn't understand all of it, but it wasn't just a lot of words strung together anymore. Now that I'd stood up for myself when the time was right, and won, Shakespeare made some sense.

Grandfather went on, "Time changes things. I find I'm changing, too." He looked down at his hands and I could see how they shook. "But I'm not yet ready to sit back, bound in shallows and miseries. There's a task I've started. I look forward to completing it. It's providing care for Robby while his father is so busy. So Robert," he nodded toward Uncle Robert, "and I have decided I'll move over with them to be there for Robby as long as he needs me. I've asked Miss Betty to cook our evening meals. We three men will manage perfectly well."

I don't know what anyone else thought about that. My eyes were on Robby's face. It was a blaze of joy. He ran and hugged Grandfather. Then he hugged Uncle Robert. Then he pounded my back and shouted, "Come on." He started dragging me across the room the way he'd dragged me through the factory that morning.

"Come home soon," Mama called. "We're about to break this party up." She smiled at Grandfather.

I grabbed the doorway and stopped Robby long enough to give Carolina the *Want to trade?* look. She nodded. She was ready to trade the teasing chants for the boys' votes. So was I. I nodded back. That shine came on her that makes people enjoy watching her. "You want to come run in the rain?" I asked her.

"No, I have to phone Lisa and Melody." She actually smiled at me.

"What did you do that for?" Robby asked as we ran across the hall. "What if she'd come?"

"Well, she didn't."

We threw our shoes and socks in one of the porch chairs. We'd been dressed up since breakfast. In August that doesn't feel normal. We ran shouting down Front Street, splashing in the gutter. Celebrating everything.